**"We had a *leak*."** She jumped the last two steps to land on the floor, jamming the roller into the pan at the foot of the ladder. "The plumber is there now, dealing with the aftermath." Reminded of the calamity in her kitchen, she turned a glower on the silent man and quirked a brow. "And you are?"

"Oh, I'm sorry." Jill rolled her eyes at Meggy and made the introductions. "Meggy Calhoun, this is Trevor Bryce. He's a writer who's interested in renting the carriage house. Mr. Bryce, Meggy is one of the owners of Palmer House. She's also the head chef."

Fascinated, Meggy watched as the stiff lawyer vanished behind a wicked smile, a flash of white teeth, and dimples. There was *nothing* stiff about the penetrating gaze that met and held hers. The deep drawl of his voice, when he said hello, reminded her of the smooth slide of the aged whiskey found in Palmer House's well-stocked bar.

She glanced at the hand he held out, and flipped up her own paint-smeared palm. "Sorry, I'm a mess."

Laugh lines crinkled the tanned skin at the corner of his eyes, and the soft core of femininity within her sighed in appreciation. She'd always had a soft spot for the Greek god type. Looking at Trevor Bryce, she had a sudden craving for feta cheese and ouzo.

# The Billionaire's Con

by

## Mackenzie Crowne

**The Billionaire's Con**

Cover Art by *Kim Mendoza*

The Wild Rose Press, Inc.
PO Box 708
Adams Basin, NY 14410-0708
Visit us at www.thewildrosepress.com

Publishing History
First Champagne Rose Edition, 2013
Digital ISBN 978-1-61217-952-0
Print ISBN 978-1-62830-077-2

Published in the United States of America

## Dedication

For Marylee. The strongest woman I know.
Love you, Mom.

Chapter One

"Palmer House was built by the town founders, Gabriel and Edith Palmer, in 1734. The new owners have been renovating the property for several months and plan to reopen a restaurant on the ground floor of the main house within the week."

Trevor Bryce Christos, CEO of Ashford Holdings and Elizabeth Ashford's right-hand man, tuned out the chatty real estate agent. He scanned the expansive, well-tended grounds, and was impressed with what he saw.

The main house sat high atop a long, climbing drive. Tucked back from the road and wearing a fresh coat of white paint, the landmark, Georgian-architecture home watched over the town of Palmerton, Massachusetts like a beloved dowager aunt. Four, weathered-brick chimneys rose from a newly shingled roof. More than a dozen mullioned windows sparkled in the morning sunlight.

Crisply sculpted shrubbery lined the grounds and drive, leading to the graceful portico covering the home's main entrance on the right side of the structure. The tang of freshly cut grass scented the air, and Trevor knew a number of country club greens keepers who would give their right arm to claim the perfect carpet of lawn, sloping toward the road.

An air of charming elegance and prosperity hung over the estate and had the slow burn of fury re-igniting in his gut. No one looking at what Megan Calhoun had accomplished would mistake her for an ordinary thief. The woman didn't waste her time on small-time swindles, and she'd been very successful in her chosen career.

That was about to change.

"In addition to getting the restaurant ready to reopen for business, the new owners had some work done to the carriage house apartment." Jill Carlson led Trevor down the gravel path to the converted carriage house. Classic rock-and-roll blasted through the open door as Trevor followed her inside.

She continued to speak, despite the blare, pitching her voice to a near yell while her eyes searched the room for the source of the music.

"Just some aesthetics, really. They've refinished the hardwood floors, painted the walls. That sort of thing." The agent gave a wave of the hand. "And the fireplace has been updated to natural gas."

A boom box sat on a counter in the tiny kitchen. She stepped to it, pressed a finger to the power button, and brought blessed silence to the apartment.

It didn't last.

"Hey!" an angry, feminine voice objected, "I was listening to that!"

Jill yelped, spinning about, and slapped a hand to her chest. "Oh, Meggy! I didn't know you were in here."

Trevor followed Jill's startled gaze—and had to lock his jaw to keep it from dropping open.

*Holy hell!*

Five feet above the floor, a tiny, annoyed blonde perched atop an ancient, wooden step-ladder. Her jean-clad behind braced against the top rung, she held a paint roller in one hand like a weapon. A glare marred the pixie-like features of her face.

Astonished at what he was seeing, he catalogued the woman's hauntingly familiar visage. Shoulder length, honey blonde waves framed the sharp lines of her cheekbones and chin. Deep blue eyes, the color of a clear sky at dusk, dominated her face. Those stunning eyes appeared huge against the porcelain of her skin, and they didn't falter under his regard. Irritation met his study with a boldness that sent a swift lash of awareness whipping across his midsection.

No wonder Elizabeth was so agitated. The woman was the image of her daughter, as if Anne hadn't died at all, but had spent the last twenty seven years growing younger, and more beautiful. Now Trevor understood why Elizabeth insisted the mysterious Megan Calhoun was Anne's granddaughter, Rachel's daughter.

He, however, didn't buy it. In his experience, true coincidence was a rarity, and Megan Calhoun's arrival at Ashford Farm last week had been a damned big coincidence.

Worth three quarters of a billion dollars, Elizabeth might seem like a plump pigeon to a cunning con-artist like Megan Calhoun, but the Ashford matriarch had never been a pushover. Despite believing this woman was her long-lost great-granddaughter, she'd given Trevor three weeks to prove her wrong. He was here to do just that. He'd see the little thief behind bars in two.

****

"What are you doing in here, Meggy?" Jill moved to stand beside the stepladder. "And why are you painting?"

Meggy frowned at the intruders, ignoring Jill for the

moment. Her gaze scanned the tall stranger. She noted his expensive suit and handsome face below a thick pelt of dark, auburn hair. Though very attractive, he had that stiff, life-is-serious-business look about him.

*Lawyer.*

Meggy sighed at the waste and turned her frown to Jill.

"I needed *something* to keep my hands occupied until I can get back into the kitchen."

Agitated as much with the delay as the mess, she flicked her hand holding the roller. A silken thread of paint danced through the air, leaving a drizzle of pale yellow across the faded denim of her favorite jeans.

*Perfect. Just perfect.*

"Get back into the kitchen?" Jill placed her hands on her hips. "I thought the kitchen was up and running."

Meggy hoisted her butt off the top of the ladder and slapped a hand to the wall when she lost her balance. From the corner of her eye, she saw the lawyer take a startled step forward. With a disgusted growl, she glared at the fresh slash of paint coating her hand, and clambered down the ladder backwards before he could reach her.

"We had a *leak*." She jumped the last two steps to land on the floor, jamming the roller into the pan at the foot of the ladder. "The plumber is there now, dealing with the aftermath." Reminded of the calamity in her kitchen, she turned a glower on the silent man and quirked a brow. "And you are?"

"Oh, I'm sorry." Jill rolled her eyes at Meggy and made the introductions. "Meggy Calhoun, this is Trevor Bryce. He's a writer who's interested in renting the carriage house. Mr. Bryce, Meggy is one of the owners of Palmer House. She's also the head chef."

Meggy watched, fascinated, as the stiff lawyer vanished behind a wicked smile, a flash of white teeth, and dimples. There was *nothing* stiff about the penetrating gaze that met and held hers. The deep drawl of his voice, when he said hello, reminded her of the smooth slide of the aged whiskey found in Palmer House's well-stocked bar.

She glanced at the hand he held out, and flipped up her own paint-smeared palm. "Sorry, I'm a mess."

Laugh lines crinkled the tanned skin at the corner of his eyes, and the soft core of femininity within her sighed in appreciation. She'd always had a soft spot for the Greek god type. Looking at Trevor Bryce, she had a sudden craving for feta cheese and ouzo.

Dark auburn hair, cut short and styled with just a hint of curl in the thick mass, framed a strong face. The olive tone of his complexion spoke of Mediterranean ancestry and complimented the sharp slash of his nose, chiseled cut of high cheekbones, and squared chin. His pale eyes were gray, without a hint of blue. They simmered with quiet humor as he returned her study. His wide mouth, though smiling, hinted at just a touch of danger.

*Danger? Where the hell had that come from?* Her gaze slid over the crisp cut of his lips once more. *Well hell, what was life without a little danger?*

"A writer, huh?" She snatched the rag she'd thrown over one of the ladder's rungs and scrubbed at the yellow streaks decorating her fingers and palm. Her gaze roamed over his lanky, six-foot frame. He wore a tailored suit that she knew, without seeing the label, would have put him back five grand, easy. "You don't have that brooding look or starving artist quality I usually associate with writers."

"I'm new to the culture." Humor continued to dance in his eyes. "But I think I could manage a brood if I put my mind to it."

Shades of the South echoed in his whiskey smooth voice. For the first time that morning, she grinned, enjoying the unexpected combination of sardonic wit and sex appeal. The rag dangled from her hand as she crossed her arms over her chest.

"Would I have read any of your work?"

"Highly doubtful." He slowly shook his head. "Since I'm working on my first novel, the jury's still out as to whether or not I have the right to call myself a writer."

"Mr. Bryce is researching life in a small town," Jill interjected. "A small, *New England* town in particular. Palmerton more than qualifies. Wouldn't you say, Meggy?"

"Excruciatingly so." Meggy had to bite her tongue to keep from laughing at Jill's anxious scowl when her lips flattened into an unhappy line. The town's only real estate agent was in full close-the-deal mode. No doubt conscious of the lack of a lease having been signed and a commission check having been written. Meggy decided to cut her some slack.

"You'll find plenty of examples of small town characteristics in Palmerton, Mr. Bryce." She winked at Jill and kicked up the Bostonian accent she'd been raised on. "And there are a number of people around town who will line up to ply you with small town yarns."

"Trevor, please." He grinned in reaction to her

exaggerated pronunciation. A *killer* grin, Meggy noted. "And are you one of those purveyors of yarns, Miss Calhoun?"

"I'm Meggy," she corrected, caught in the dazzle of white teeth and sparkling gray eyes. "And, no way." She laughed. "I avoid the grapevine at every opportunity."

"The grapevine?"

She sent Jill a thin smile. "The grapevine is Palmerton's version of the information superhighway. It's an organized effort."

He shook his head, confusion puckering his brow

With a nervous chuckle, Jill did her best to redirect the conversation. "The gossip mill is a fact of life in Palmerton, Mr. Bryce, but it's harmless." She paused for a beat. "For the most part. Why don't I show you the apartment so we can get out of Meggy's way?"

Meggy fought a smile as he turned in a slow circle, taking in the first floor studio.

He flicked a long fingered hand in the direction of the queen bed, prominent in one corner. "The bedroom?"

Jill nodded, and pointed to the staircase along the opposite wall. "The second floor is a small loft bedroom."

He didn't bother checking the loft. "The place looks like it will suit my needs. I'll take it."

"Well," Jill sputtered, shooting a surprised glance at Meggy before turning back to him. "Well, then. Why don't we head back to my office to take care of the paperwork?"

Trevor nodded. "That works for me."

"Do you have any questions before we leave?" Jill sashayed toward the door.

"Only one." He didn't move, and Jill stumbled to a stop when he asked Meggy, "Where can I find you, Meggy Calhoun? One never knows when one may need some painting or yarn spinning advice."

Meggy blinked at the sultry southern drawl, as well as his dark and intimate smile. She returned the smile, deciding she'd been right about that dangerous tilt after all. The man was definitely dangerous.

She jerked a thumb over her shoulder at the open doorway. "I live in the main house." Her smile morphed into a grin at the thought of her tiny, third-floor apartment. "Top floor. Penthouse."

"Then I'll be seeing you. It's been my pleasure." He held out his hand and she didn't hesitate in offering hers. His warm, slightly roughened fingers folded around hers. She jerked back her hand almost immediately.

*Whoa! What was that?* Her palm and fingers tingled as though she'd just grabbed hold of a live wire.

His pale gaze swept over her once more. He smiled and followed Jill outside.

Chapter Two

"Cara! Are you here?" Meggy's voice echoed off the gleaming, hardwood floors of the large studio. An unfinished canvas rested on the easel in the corner, and she wandered over to study it. The strong scent of turpentine assailed her senses.

She tossed her purse onto the couch behind her, turning her back on the disturbing letter tucked in the inside pocket of the bag. *Out of sight, out of mind? Yeah, right.* She'd been doing her best not to think about that letter since first reading the damn thing three weeks ago—without success.

If not for that letter, she would never have made that asinine trip to Martha's Vineyard. The only thing she'd accomplished on her trip to Ashford Farm was feeling like a coward. The sensation didn't sit well with her.

Instinct told her the smart thing to do would be to burn the letter, forget about Martha's Vineyard and rich old ladies, and focus on making Palmer House into the North Shore's most successful new restaurant. But her instincts had been on the fritz since the moment she'd learned of the letter's existence.

"Hey! Mrs. Finnegan! Where are you?" she called out.

"It's so weird to hear myself addressed as a Mrs."

Meggy turned—and sputtered with laughter.

Descending the spiral staircase from the second floor, her newly married friend looked tanned, rested, and otherwise gorgeous in spite of the ridiculous, oversized sombrero balanced on her head. "Nice hat," Meggy quipped.

"I think it makes a statement." Cara reached the bottom step and walked toward her.

"It makes a statement, all right." When Cara stopped, Meggy flicked at the floppy brim. "It confirms that even intelligent people can be suckered into buying cheesy souvenirs while on their honeymoon."

Cara grinned, her green eyes sparkling. She lifted the three-foot-wide hat from her head, and dropped it onto Meggy's. "It's not a cheesy souvenir. It's a gift for my maid of honor."

"Oh, goody." She studied her reflection in the gilded mirror gracing the aged-brick of the studio's back wall. She looked as ridiculous as Cara had in the oversized hat, but that was where the similarities ended. Behind her, Cara stood almost a head taller than her own five-foot-two. Her friend's vivid green eyes, golden tanned skin, and long, riotously curling, dark red hair were a bohemian contrast to Meggy's pale, pixie looks. Looking at them, strangers might assign personalities to go along with those contrasting exteriors—bold and daring to the statuesque, dark-haired bohemian, sweet and unassuming to the petite, pixie-faced blonde.

And they'd be wrong, as the exact opposite was true.

Meggy pushed up the brim of the hat, grimacing at her absurd reflection. "Any other maid of honor would expect something shiny with a big chunk of sparkle, but not me." She shook her head. "There's nothing I've wanted more than a woven hat that can double as a canopy."

Cara laughed, and reached into the pocket of her paint-spattered shirt. A royal-blue box appeared in her hand. She waggled it back and forth over Meggy's shoulder. "This must be for some *other* maid of honor then."

The sombrero went flying when Meggy whipped around. She snatched the jeweler's box from Cara's fingers.

"The wicker hat is from me." Cara pointed to the box. "That's from Finn."

Meggy lifted the lid. Her breath caught as sunlight flashed off the bluish-purple stone in the dazzling pendant.

"Oh, Cara." She sucked air, dazzled by the beauty of it. "I was just kidding." Cara's smile was soft as Meggy lifted the silver and tanzanite necklace from its satin bed, and held it up to the light. "It's too much."

"I told Finn you'd say that." Cara took the necklace to clasp it at the back of Meggy's neck. "But he insisted. He dragged me all over Mexico looking for it."

"I appreciate the effort." Meggy grinned and fingered the beautiful bauble. "Thank him for me, Cara. And tell him I'm keeping it, even though it had to be wicked expensive, because I deserve it."

Cara laughed, but her face remained serious. "Yes, you do."

The tendons in her throat tightened, and she waved her hand in front of her face. She spun. "Okay, cut it out before you make me cry." She nodded toward the canvas in the corner, all bold colors and sultry slashes. "I don't have to ask if you enjoyed the honeymoon.

What will you call it when it's done? Satisfied Woman?"

Cara shrugged, eyeing the canvas. "What can I say? My groom knows his stuff." Utter happiness sparkled in her eyes, even as wistfulness drew out her sigh. "As far as being satisfied, my memories will have to sustain me for tonight. Finn's out of town."

"Suck it up, Mrs. Finnegan." She attempted to tease her friend out of her doldrums. "You'll just have to rough it like the rest of us women who aren't having newlywed sex with the town stud."

"Jealousy is an ugly emotion," Cara countered in a sweet voice. "It'll give you wrinkles."

"There's always Botox." She grinned at Cara's chuckle. "Of course I'm jealous. The closest I've come to a meaningful relationship lately is when old man Watson winked at me in the hardware store last week."

The memory of Trevor Bryce's gray eyes and sexy, dimpled smile flashed through her mind, and a lovely little shimmer of pleasure tightened her belly. She shook the vision clear.

"It doesn't matter anyway. Palmer House is taking all my energy these days. I'm too busy to worry over my non-existent love life." Her gaze strayed to the purse on the couch where her birth mother's letter waited. She scowled, grumbling, "Or anything else."

"What's wrong?" Cara's eyes narrowed. "Is there a problem at Palmer House?"

Meggy shook her head. "There was a plumbing issue, but it's been handled." Squeezing her eyes shut, she blew out a breath. She knew she looked guilty when her eyes opened to meet Cara's watchful gaze. "Remember when I mentioned that I was thinking about asking Mom and Dad about my birth parents?"

"You talked to them about your adoption?"

Meggy nodded.

"And?"

"And I wish I hadn't."

Cara's brow furrowed in concern. "Were they upset that you have questions?"

"No." She scooped her purse from the couch and rummaged through it. "No, they were fine with it. Better than fine, actually. They were great. Dad gave me the documents from the adoption, and they told me everything they knew. Which wasn't much. There was no information about my birth father, but my birth mother's name is Rachel Hadley." She pulled the envelope from her purse and held it out. "And then there was this."

Cara took the envelope. "What is it?"

"A letter. Rachel Hadley mailed it to my parents four years ago. She asked that they give it to me if I ever had questions about where I came from." She gestured at the letter. "Go ahead. Read it."

Cara pulled the single folded page from the envelope and lowered to the couch.

There was no reason to join Cara as she read, she knew the words by heart. There were precious few of them, and none that answered the nagging question of why Rachel had given her up. Neither did they give her any hope of ever finding her birth mother. Instead, the short missive had the tone of finality, as if Rachel were tying up a loose end. But as loose ends went, Rachel's letter delivered a bombshell.

"Holy crap!" Cara looked up to meet her gaze.

"Yeah, that was pretty much my reaction too." She

crossed her arms under her breasts.

"Elizabeth Ashford is your biological great-grandmother?" Cara looked stunned.

As stunned as she'd been when she found out.

"Elizabeth Ashford of the Martha's Vineyard Ashfords?"

"The very same."

"Holy crap," Cara repeated.

"Tell me about it. You should see her house, Cara. It's a frigging mansion."

"You've met her already? What's she like? What did she say when you introduced yourself? Did she know about you?"

She jammed the heels of her palms into her eye sockets. "Since I haven't actually met her yet, I can't answer any of those questions."

"Wait. What? I thought you said you went to her house."

"I did. I just didn't meet her." She dropped her arms and moved to join Cara on the couch, slouching back against the pillows.

"You've lost me," Cara's eyebrows dipped.

"I asked Justin to check her out for me." She exhaled an audible sigh. Justin Cooper remained her friend long after their short romance ended three years earlier. As a cop, he had access to information others didn't, and he hadn't hesitated when she asked him for information on the wealthy real estate matriarch. "One of the things he found out," she added with a guilty grimace, "was that Elizabeth Ashford was in the process of looking to hire a chef for her estate on the Vineyard."

"Oh, Meggy," Cara groaned. "Tell me you didn't."

"Okay, but I'd be lying." She scoffed at Cara's

pained expression. "Oh, come on. How could you expect me to learn something like that and not take advantage of the situation? Talk about serendipity. I applied for the job, and a couple of days later, the housekeeper called me for an interview."

Cara snorted, half laugh, half groan. "You actually went through with the interview?"

"How else was I going to get inside? I'd already come all that way, and I couldn't exactly tell them I wasn't really interested in the job, just a chance to look around. Anyway, I almost chickened out once I'd seen the place, but I couldn't, you know? So, I let them know I was there. A bodyguard met me at the door."

"A bodyguard?"

"Yeah. Well, he didn't introduce himself as the bodyguard or anything, but I could tell that's what he was. He was huge, and he had this wicked-looking scar across one eyebrow." She made a slashing motion to emphasize her words. "He stood there staring with these arms, as thick as hams, crossed over his chest in one of those moves guys make when they want to intimidate someone. He had the move down pat, believe me. I didn't think he was going to let me in."

"But he did?"

"The housekeeper did. She thought I was a lunatic, I'm sure. I told her I'd only come to let her know I wouldn't be available for the job. The interview lasted about five seconds."

"Sometimes you scare me, Meggy."

"Sometimes I scare myself." They shared a grin.

"Why didn't you just explain who you were and ask to meet your great-grandmother?"

She frowned, tugging on the hem of her shirt. "I

was scared."

"Scared?" Cara gaped at her. "Meggy Calhoun, the Palmerton pit bull, was too scared to meet with a little old lady?" She snorted an exaggerated sniff. "Right."

Meggy narrowed her eyes at her friend. The nickname was warranted, and normally hearing it gave her a laugh, but her natural assertiveness had deserted her completely with one look at the Ashford Estate. Though she'd forced herself to go inside, she'd run like a coward at the first opportunity. It was embarrassing. And worse, she knew she'd do it again in a heartbeat.

"I stood there, looking around that house. You should have seen it, Cara. The artwork in one room alone could fund several third-world countries for years. Why would anyone walk away from all of that? What kind of woman is Elizabeth Ashford that her own granddaughter didn't want anything to do with her, that she chose to give me up rather than go to her grandmother for help?"

She didn't give Cara a chance to answer. "The Ashfords have the kind of money you only read about. Does that kind of wealth warp people? Elizabeth Ashford isn't just going to accept me with open arms if I show up on her doorstep. Do I really want to put myself in a position where I'm forced to defend myself, when if I do nothing at all, I won't have to?"

With a sigh, she sat forward to rest her elbows on her knees. She glanced over her shoulder at Cara. "Anyway, I have too much at stake right now, too many other things to think about. Palmer House has to be my only focus. It's too important to me not to give it my full attention. When things calm down..." She shrugged. "I'll deal with Elizabeth Ashford then."

Chapter Three

Trevor let himself inside his Beacon Street penthouse and shrugged out of his suit jacket. He tossed the keys to the carriage house onto the entry table as he passed. His briefcase joined his jacket on the couch as he kicked off his shoes. In stocking feet, he padded into the kitchen to grab a beer from the refrigerator before heading to the couch.

He'd signed a six-month lease on the studio apartment, much to Jill Carlson's disappointment. She'd been pushing for a full year. The best he'd been able to offer was the possibility he may extend it at a later date. It wasn't going to happen, but she didn't need to know that. She'd taken what she could get.

The two-bedroom apartment on the grounds of Palmer House couldn't have been more perfect for his needs. He had little interest in the amenities of the converted garage. With any luck, he wouldn't be there long enough to unpack.

The rent hadn't been cheap. The ladies of Palmer House had set a high price for the pleasure of renting the small apartment. Subsidizing their income until the restaurant took off, Jill said. Just the cost of doing business, Trevor reminded himself.

He propped his feet on the etched-stone coffee table, ignoring the briefcase full of files while he sipped at his beer. There was no point in trying to work, not when a tiny woman with a cap of blonde waves and crystal blue eyes kept drifting through his thoughts—a woman he planned to destroy to keep Elizabeth from being hurt, yet again.

Though there was no blood connection between him and the Ashford matriarch, Elizabeth was family. He'd do whatever it took to protect her. It had been Elizabeth with whom he'd felt an instant connection when his widowed father married her daughter, Anne, when Trevor was eight. That connection grew to love less than a year later, when his father and Anne were killed by a drunk driver, and Trevor was left orphaned. Elizabeth won his undying love and gratitude with her announcement that he belonged to her now.

At the time, he'd been too young, and too grief stricken, to understand the true scope of Elizabeth's grief. A grief compounded when Anne's daughter, eighteen-year-old Rachel, walked away from Ashford Farm, never to be heard from again. Elizabeth's love eventually healed his own sense of loss, but years passed before he came to understand just how much she still suffered over the loss of Anne and Rachel.

Elizabeth spent a fortune over the years, searching for any word of Rachel, without success. It was as if his step-sister had vanished. Then, five years ago, a young woman bearing a strong resemblance to Rachel showed up at the farm, claiming to be her daughter. Elizabeth had been ecstatic.

Only when the idea of a DNA test had been introduced was the truth exposed. The woman disappeared as quickly as she had appeared. The experience left Elizabeth devastated, and still had the ability to make Trevor's blood boil.

He wasn't about to see the situation repeated. Megan Calhoun hadn't made any type of claim, hadn't requested to meet Elizabeth. She'd stayed less than five minutes, and yet, her visit lasted long enough for Elizabeth to see her.

He yanked at the knot of his tie and slipped the top button of his dress shirt, loosening the constriction at his throat. Her excuse of wanting to turn down the chef's position in person was laughable. Now that he'd seen the setup at Palmer House, he was even more convinced she hadn't come to the farm because of any position. She already had one.

No, Megan Calhoun had gone to Ashford Farm to get a look at the place and had scored the accidental bonus of having her remarkable resemblance to Anne noted. He'd bet money on it.

He had to hand it to her, her cover was good. He hadn't found a whiff of corruption in her background. Everything he'd discovered so far corroborated the image she projected of a small town girl from a loving home. He'd found no record of an adoption, which would have at least opened the door to the possibility that Rachel could have been her birth mother.

Still, there was always the possibility of a private adoption. If that were the case, he'd need to dig a little deeper to find a record. He didn't expect to find any such record, however, and it would be interesting to see how she explained away loving parents when she made her claim.

She was ambitious enough to start up a business in an industry that saw most of its daring entrepreneurs fail within the first year. And owning and operating Palmer House was no small ambition. The property carried a hefty mortgage, incentive enough to have a smart woman looking for other means of funding.

He rubbed a palm over his jaw. The partnership of Palmer House interested him. Megan, Meggy, he corrected himself, was one of three equal partners in the venture with sisters Shannon and Cara O'Shea. By all accounts, Shannon looked to be what she appeared—a single mom, struggling to get by, who just happened to have some expertise in the field of restaurant management. Unlike Meggy and Cara, however, her name wasn't on the mortgage.

The third partner, Cara O'Shea Finnegan was the new bride of ex-pro quarterback, Michael Finnegan, and was a successful artist in her own right. Finn was said to have the Midas touch when it came to business investments, and was worth millions. His artist wife raked in the cash with each pricey canvas sold.

On the surface, the Finnegans had too much to lose by involving themselves in an illegal scam, even one worth millions. Could Meggy Calhoun have conned the football star and his artist wife, the way she was planning to con Elizabeth?

A simple DNA test would settle the matter with a minimum of fuss, but he was holding that option in reserve. She'd yet to play her hand and he needed her to if he was going to prosecute her to the fullest extent of the law.

In the meantime, his ruse as a writer doing research would allow him to move around the edges of her life without suspicion. As far as anyone knew, Trevor Bryce had come to town to do research for a book. Any questions he asked would be chalked up to literary curiosity.

He dropped his head against the couch back with a satisfied grunt. If his questions about a certain, petite blonde appeared a little too personal? Well, what red-blooded man *wouldn't* want to know more about a woman who looked like Meggy Calhoun?

\*\*\*\*

"*That's* our new tenant?"

Meggy laughed at her friend's excited reaction.

Whereas Cara was tall and dark, her sisters, Shan and Erin, were both petite, strawberry-blondes. All three shared the same piercing, green eyes. Just now, Shan's sparkling, green gaze was incredulous. They shared a grin. Their shoulders bumped as they leaned closer to the window to enjoy the sight of Trevor Bryce unloading a black Mercedes in the driveway below.

She sighed, watching him carry a large box up the pathway to the carriage house door.

He bent to set the box on the stoop, straightened, and shoved a hand into the pocket of worn jeans to pull out a key.

"Don't you just love when life works out so nicely?" She shot Shan a grin. "A monthly rent check with a butt you can bounce a quarter off."

Shan's breath barked out in a shocked cough.

"Oh, come on, Shan. Look at him." She leaned closer to the window until her nose was all but pressed to the glass. "If you tell me you're not swallowing back drool, we're using his first check to get you some professional help."

"God, Meggy." Shan laughed. "You're like a female construction worker."

Her gaze never left the man on the pathway below. God, he was glorious. "No, if I were a female construction worker, I'd open this window and call out lewd comments, instead of just admiring from afar."

Shan snickered.

Meggy stepped back from the window when Trevor disappeared behind the carriage house door. "So, what's on your agenda this morning?"

Hot coffee warmed her as she leaned against the counter sipping while Shan outlined her busy morning. Although they minded each other's privacy in their individual living spaces, they'd gotten into the habit of catching up on the day's business over coffee or iced-tea in Shan's second floor kitchen. The routine reminded her of when they'd been kids. She'd spent many an hour in the O'Shea kitchen with Cara and her sisters. It was there she'd learned her love of the culinary arts.

"What are you doing up this early? I thought you'd sleep in today so you'd be fresh for tonight." Shan pressed a hand to her stomach. "I can't believe tonight's the night. I'm a bundle of nerves."

She was too excited to be nervous. Or was it her nerves that had her so excited she thought she'd never breathe at a normal rate again? The renovations had taken time, and the waiting had been excruciating. Now, at long last, they were finally ready. Palmer House would officially reopen tonight, and her dream of running her own kitchen would be a reality.

"I'm headed into Boston, to the fish market." A glance at the clock had her dumping the dregs of coffee from her mug. "And I'd better get going before there's nothing left and we end up having to serve frozen fish sticks to Wallis."

Shan grimaced at the mention of the well-known food critic. "Do you think he'll make an appearance tonight? He hasn't made a reservation."

"He won't be able to help himself. He'll consider it his sworn duty to review my worthiness in my own kitchen."

"The man does seem to have a personal interest in your career. I think he has a secret crush on you." Shan waggled her eyebrows and then added a smirk.

She snorted her disdain. Wallis confused his considerable influence in the local culinary community for sexual magnetism. In her opinion, he had too much of the former and *none* of the latter. *The jerk.*

"Whatever his agenda, a positive review will put us on the map. I plan to knock his socks off." She hooked the strap of her purse over her shoulder and headed for the private staircase to the restaurant below. "I'll see you in a couple of hours."

At the bottom of the stairs, she paused to look around at the gleaming industrial kitchen, enjoying the giddy surge of pure possessiveness. This, at last, was hers. At the spotless stoves and ovens, on the yards of stainless steel counters, she would make her mark, and the result would taste like ambrosia.

The room was empty now, but in her mind she could already see the choreographed dance she and her staff would perform here in just a few hours. She couldn't wait to slip on her smock and dazzle the diners with the results of the performance.

Chapter Four

Meggy was smiling as she stepped outside, mentally running through her to-do list. One look at Trevor Bryce, however, rummaging through the trunk of his big, dark car, sent thoughts of the day's many tasks flying right out of her mind. *Oh, yeah.* She strolled over to stand behind him. The man had a world-class butt.

The tailored suit was absent today. His long legs were caressed by a pair of softly faded jeans. A black T-shirt stretched across the subtle musculature of his wide shoulders. Short sleeves revealed surprisingly ripped biceps when he hefted a duffle bag from the trunk to hold it dangling over his shoulder with one hand. He pivoted, and his gray gaze widened as it collided with hers.

"All moved in?" She gave him her most cheerful smile, hoping there was no drool on her chin.

"This is the last of it." He stepped back and shut the trunk with a quiet click. Squatting, he lifted one of two boxes from the ground. He tucked it under his free arm.

Without a word, she stooped and picked up the remaining box. Her brow furrowed at the surprising weight, and she shifted the heavy carton in her arms. "What have you got in here, barbells?"

"Leave it. I'll get it in a minute."

"A minute is about all I have to do my duty as a good neighbor and help you move in your stuff." She laughed when he hesitated. "I've got it, Trevor, but it's not getting any lighter."

At her challenging smile, he moved aside to let her pass. "After you."

She stepped through the open door of the carriage house.

He brushed by her, dropping the duffle bag on an oversized chair. He set the box he carried on the small kitchen table. "Here, let me have that." He stepped close to relieve her of the second box, setting it aside as though it weighed nothing.

She expected him to step away from her then. Her brows lifted in surprise when he turned back, standing close enough that she could feel the heat radiating from his big body.

*God, he smelled richer than her double-chocolate-brownie-cheesecakes baking in the ovens.* The surprising intimacy of standing in the sphere of that heat, of *his* heat, was startling, and delicious. Before she gave in to the insane urge to close the remaining distance between them, she forced herself to step back—bumping against the edge of the kitchen counter.

A self-conscious chuckle escaped, but died on her lips when she looked into his eyes. She blinked at the hot flare of male interest in the gray depths only inches from hers. Her belly lurched on a crazy bump when he reached out a hand. The breath caught in her throat at the slow brush of his fingertips dancing across her cheekbone then continuing down to track the curve of her jaw.

His hand dropped to his side and he stepped back. "Thanks for the help."

Meggy could only stare, wide-eyed. *Holy crap!*

*Okay, this is just weird.* That odd zapping sensation she remembered from yesterday had her entire body tingling with warm current today.

The rumble of a diesel motor, as the first of today's delivery trucks ambled by the carriage house, had reason returning to her muddled brain. At least enough so that she managed to resist grabbing hold of Trevor Bryce and attempting to discover what it was about the guy that had her insides jumping around like crazed three year olds in a candy store.

Palmer House was opening in just a few hours, for heaven's sake. Fantasizing about having wild monkey-sex with a guy she just met probably wasn't a good idea today.

"It looks like you have some unpacking to do." Flustered, she gave an expressive wave of her hand.

"Not all that much." He leaned against the counter, slipping both hands into the front pockets of his jeans.

Though his stance was casual, she was gratified to hear the gruffness of his voice. It hinted that she hadn't been the only one to have her circuits fried by that simple touch.

"I'll be commuting back and forth between here and home for the duration," he continued. "There will be some things I'll have to see to occasionally, so I only brought what I couldn't do without."

"Where's home?"

"Work takes me up and down the East Coast. I spend a good portion of my time in Boston and Atlanta, and I have a place on Virginia Beach."

"What kind of business? You said you were new to writing." Her gaze slid to the open door and the big Mercedes parked outside. "What have you been doing to feed yourself up until now? Whatever it is, it must be lucrative for you to afford such a sweet ride."

"I'm in finance and real estate."

She wondered at the sudden intensity in his gaze.

"My father left me some money when he died. I was just a kid, but my guardian invested it wisely. When I was old enough to try my hand, I found I have a knack for investing myself."

"I'm sorry, Trevor." She resisted the urge to reach out and rest her hand on his arm, unwilling to risk reheating those circuits that had just begun to cool.

Confusion wrinkled his brow. "You're sorry I've got a knack with investments?"

A fleeting smile tugged at her lips at his dry tone. "I'm sorry about your father. I've never lost anyone I love, and I can't imagine losing my dad." The movement was barely perceptible, but he stiffened.

He was silent for a long moment, his gaze holding hers.

As she watched, the warmth in his eyes cooled by more than a few degrees. She wasn't sure what she'd said to upset him. All she knew was that something had shifted. Those soft gray eyes weren't at all warm now. Instead, they looked like cold slate.

"It was a long time ago," he finally replied, his tone cool and sharp.

Embarrassed, and oddly hurt, she wasn't sure how to respond to his lightning fast change of mood. People reacted differently to grief. It appeared to make Trevor Bryce cranky.

"Well." She cleared her throat and pasted a smile on her mouth that she knew didn't reach her eyes. "I'll leave you to your unpacking." She moved then, backing out the open door and down the gravel walkway, calling back to him where he stood in the open door frame. "It'll be a mad house around here today. We're reopening the restaurant tonight. I'm not sure you can still get a dinner reservation, that's Shan's department, but stop by the kitchen and we'll fix you up."

She spun on her heel, scrambling into the old pickup truck parked beneath the portico. Her eyes found his reflection in the rearview mirror and she sighed. The sudden chilling of his manner was probably for the best. She had too much at stake to let herself be side-tracked by anything right now, and that included the irresistible Greek god in her carriage house.

**** 

Trevor watched the truck disappear around the corner. Well, hell. He'd bungled that. He had no answer for why he'd touched her. Temporary insanity, maybe. Setting aside the possibility she was a con artist, he didn't even know the woman. But suddenly, discovering if her skin was as soft as it appeared seemed as necessary as taking his next breath. Warmed silk had met his fingertips, and he couldn't help wondering about other places on her sleek little body, even softer places that only a lover would uncover.

He shook his head in self-disgust and shut the door.

As for freezing her out, it had either been that, or give in to the urge to kiss the little thief. Hell, she was good, all gentle teasing and easy smiles. She'd looked so sincere with her soft words and sympathetic blue eyes. If he wasn't careful, he'd find himself under the pixie chef's spell. Physically, he was already half way there, reacting to her teasing charm like a randy teenager. His fingers felt singed just from touching her cheek. If he ever really put his hands on her, he'd probably combust.

The woman wasn't stupid. She'd sensed his cold fury, and had backed away, literally as well as figuratively. The smile she'd offered along with the invitation to come by the kitchen later hadn't been the open fairy grin he'd come to associate with her. Instead, she'd worn the tepid expression with which one greeted a stranger.

If he was going to discover her secrets in the limited time available, he'd need to do a better job of concealing his feelings. And he'd have to repair the damage he'd done with his cold response.

The glazed look in her eyes as he'd explored the texture of her cheek proved she was no more physically immune to him than he was to her. He'd use their mutual attraction to soften her up, if it became necessary. That he was hoping it did, he refused to consider too closely.

In the meantime, he'd take her up on her invitation to visit her kitchen this evening.

Chapter Five

From the shadows, Trevor studied Meggy directing the organized chaos that was the Palmer House kitchen. Gone was the gently teasing woman from that morning. In her place was a tiny, blonde general. As she snapped out orders, it was clear she'd chosen her staff well. The half dozen line cooks toiled about their individual stations while the wait staff moved efficiently between kitchen and dining areas, bearing the fruits of the their labors.

The door to the dining room swung in constant motion. Trevor raised an appreciative brow when it opened to admit a stunning, six-foot redhead. The pictures he'd seen of Finn's new bride hadn't come close to doing her justice. Cara O'Shea Finnegan was a knockout. A moment passed before he noticed the blonde bruiser she tugged along in her wake.

"Look who I found skulking at the bar." Cara's wide grin matched the bruiser's.

Meggy's eyes widened, and a squeal of delight escaped her lips as she launched herself across the space and into the man's arms. "Justin! What are you doing here?"

"Did you think I'd miss your big night?" Holding her pressed against his large frame, the man named Justin grinned and fingered the lapel of her smock. "You know I can't resist a woman in uniform."

"You can't resist women period." She laughed.

He shrugged unapologetically. "That little favor you asked of me has been driving me crazy. You didn't return my last call, so I thought I'd kill two birds by surprising you. Now, when are you going to tell me what that was all about?"

Trevor wondered what kind of favor she'd asked of the man. Was the big, blonde bruiser a partner in crime, or just another victim? Following the progress of Justin's hand as it brushed down Meggy's slim body to pat at her bottom with a casualness that spoke of familiarity, Trevor hoped he was guilty as sin. He'd enjoy seeing the bastard behind bars.

"I promise to satisfy your infamous curiosity as soon as possible, but I'm a little busy at the moment." Meggy batted at the hand on her backside, and with a light shove, pushed her way out of his arms. Then she tugged at the hem of her smock. "Now get the hell out of my kitchen so I can dazzle the masses with my superior culinary skills."

Justin's dark eyes were full of laughter as he tipped up her chin with a fingertip. "I'll hold you to that promise. Break a leg, Meg." He dropped a kiss on her mouth before making his way back to the dining room.

The door swung open behind him to reveal the head of a dark-haired waitress. "Shan said to tell you they just seated Wallis."

"Thanks, Simone." Meggy pressed a hand to her stomach.

For the first time since he'd entered the kitchen, he saw nerves dance across her face. He stepped from the shadows, and she glanced his way. The subtle stiffening of her spine when he moved toward her told him he was

31

responsible for at least a portion of those nerves.

"Hello, Trevor. Have you come for dinner?" She pivoted to approve the presentation of a shrimp dish with a nod to a line chef.

He stopped several feet away. "Yes, but I don't want to be in the way."

She gestured to a small table tucked into the corner. "You won't be. Cara, this is Trevor Bryce." She spared him a cool smile. "He's the new tenant in the carriage house. Trevor, this is my friend and one of my partners, Cara Finnegan."

Trevor shook the hand Cara held out. "It's a pleasure meeting you, Mrs. Finnegan. And congratulations. I read about your marriage in the paper a couple of weeks ago."

"Thank you." Cara's smile was warm and genuine. "I hope you'll be comfortable in the carriage house."

"I'm sure I will." He turned back to Meggy. "Are you sure I won't be in the way here? I could take a plate and go."

"You won't be in the way," she repeated.

He was relieved to see that her smile lost some of its chill.

"What can we get you?"

"Surprise me." He smiled before heading to the corner to await his meal, taking a chair that allowed him a view of the busy kitchen.

"Where's Finn?"

"He's at the bar." Cara snagged a baby carrot from a bowl on the counter and nibbled delicately. "He said, and I quote, 'Wild horses couldn't drag me into the pit bull's kitchen tonight'."

Meggy laughed. "He's such a weenie."

Cara popped the remainder of the carrot into her mouth. "I'll enjoy telling him you said so."

Meggy nodded her approval of a tray of appetizers then frowned at the presentation of a plate of lamb chops with fresh mint. Her stocky, dark-haired *sous* chef stepped over to snatch the plate from the prep table and returned it to the line chef without a word.

"Finn wanted me to give you something."

Meggy turned with raised brows. "Oh, yeah? What?"

"Just this." Cara leaned forward to give Meggy a smacking kiss on the mouth. She stepped back, grinning.

Meggy smirked, crossing white-sleeved arms over her chest. "I always knew there had to be *something* wrong with your football stud." Her eyes sparkled, and her voice was a slicing purr. "Turns out he's a lousy kisser."

Trevor chuckled as they shared a grin.

Any response Cara would have made was lost with Simone's return. "Order up for Wallis."

"I'll get out of your way." Cara squeezed Meggy's arm. "Knock him dead, babe!"

Trevor noted the immediate tension that filled the air, and Meggy's face, with Simone's announcement. When Cara passed him to reenter the dining room, he delayed her with a raised brow. "Who's Wallis?"

"Food critic." She grimaced. "The guy knows his stuff professionally. Personally, he's a total cretin."

Trevor nodded his understanding, and when the door closed behind her, he settled back to watch Meggy. No nerves now. The little general was back. She barked instructions while Simone gave her the critic's order.

Working silently with a minimum of movement,

Meggy's face was a mask of concentration. Her staff left her alone, and their easy chatter quieted. Eleven tense minutes later, she stepped back and studied the plate critically. She handed it to Simone. Without a word, the waitress returned to the dining room.

As he watched, Meggy closed her eyes and took a deep, cleansing breath. When her eyes opened again, she glanced around at her staff, all of whom waited with a sense of expectation. A slow grin spread over her face.

"Thanks, Cal." She took the glass of wine her *sous* chef handed her, tapping it against the one he held. "If I know Wallis, he'll be having a gastronomical orgasm in about two minutes." The staff snickered, and she grinned before taking a sip of the golden wine. Setting aside the glass, she rubbed her hands together. "Okay. What's next?"

From across the room, Trevor could all but see the tension drain out of her as she refocused on her kitchen. She had complete confidence in her professional abilities, and from the reactions of her staff, they did as well. A glimmer of respect bumped up against the distrust he felt, and he didn't try to fight it.

Instead, he drew her attention. "Meggy," he called out softly.

She swung around at the sound of her name, blinking at him.

He was amused to realize she'd forgotten his presence.

"Oh! I'm sorry, Trevor." Her hand fluttered then dropped to her side. "I was going to fix you a plate."

"No rush." He made his smile wicked. "I've been enjoying the show."

A slight blush rose on her cheekbones, but there

was pleasure in her smile when she turned away to prepare him a plate.

"I've decided what I want."

"Oh?" She looked back at him over one shoulder.

"I'll have whatever Wallis is having." He winked. With wry acceptance, he welcomed the hot lash of desire that accompanied her delighted laughter.

\*\*\*\*

Meggy let herself out the back door of the kitchen, exhausted but exhilarated. She'd done it! Palmer House was going to be a success. The reviews would tell, but she knew in her heart they were on their way.

She headed for the old swing at the back of the property, too wired to sleep just yet. It had been quite a day. Trevor's swarthy image shimmered through her brain. Oh, yeah. Quite a day.

When she'd pulled out of the driveway this morning, she hadn't known what to think. The mixed messages she'd gotten from him during the few minutes they'd spent in the carriage house had left her rattled and a little bit hurt. Which was stupid. She hardly knew the guy. So, they'd shared a moment. That didn't mean she had any business feeling hurt and bewildered when he gave her that hard look and spoke in that cold voice.

Obviously, the memory of his father's death was a touchy subject. But by the time he'd come into the kitchen tonight, the charming man she'd met the day before was back in place. Despite her opening night jitters, his warm smile made her heart pound in her chest, and a warmth washed through her that had nothing to do with the heat from the ovens.

Introducing him to Cara, she'd been more than a little disturbed to find herself holding her breath. Even the most controlled of men tended to trip over their own tongues when faced with the statuesque and curvy Cara. It had never failed to amuse her before, but for reasons she couldn't explain, she didn't think she'd enjoy seeing the urbane Trevor Bryce making a fool of himself over her friend.

When he'd greeted Cara politely and respectfully, without any of the usual male speculation Cara normally inspired, she was more relieved than she should have been. And when he'd immediately turned back, concerned only that he was going to be in the way, she'd wanted to step into his arms and hug him, right there in front of her staff.

She frowned into the darkness. Trevor Bryce was going to be a problem.

"What's with the frown?"

Meggy yelped as Trevor stepped out of the shadows. "I thought you'd be on top of the world considering the raving I heard in your dining room tonight."

"God! You scared me!" She slapped a hand to her chest.

"Sorry." He shrugged. "Couldn't sleep."

Her heart pounded, due as much to his presence as from the scare he'd given her. "Me either." She breathed deep in an attempt to calm her quaking nerves. "I've been dreaming of tonight my whole life."

"So, how does it feel? Realizing your dream?"

Her smile was wide and unapologetic. "It feels frigging awesome!"

He threw back his head on a throaty laugh and with his humor came the return of that odd zinging across her nerve endings. His pale eyes continued to sparkle as he wound down.

"Frigging awesome is a good thing."

"A very good thing," she agreed, grinning.

"Well." He rolled his shoulders. "I don't want to intrude. I was just enjoying the night air."

"Trevor." She took a step toward him before he could turn away, and he met her gaze with a questioning lift of his brow. "I'm sorry about earlier. I didn't mean to upset you by reminding you of your father's death."

"You're sorry," he muttered. His gaze roamed her face as though searching for something elusive. They were standing close, just a foot separating them, and his hand came up to cup her cheek. "Who are you, Meggy Calhoun?"

The tingling heat was familiar now. She wasn't sure what he was asking, and so answered the only way she knew. "I'm the head chef of the best damned restaurant in the Boston metroplex."

"You are that." A dimple popped with his smile. His gaze dropped to her mouth. "And so much more, I think."

"Oh," she breathed when he did what she wanted to do, and closed the distance between them. Her breath came out in a whoosh as he leaned down and covered her mouth with his.

She immediately felt like she was drowning in a vat of warmed honey. His tongue slid along hers in a tempting caress, and she followed his lead like a willing student.

Oh, yeah. The man had secret weapons. And he had aimed and fired this one with the precision of a Special Forces operative. If he didn't stop soon, she wasn't going to survive his mission. The question was, did she want to survive?

*Survival is overrated*, the greedy little voice in her head insisted.

Sliding deeper into his embrace was the most natural thing she'd ever done. Of their own accord, her hands slipped up over broad shoulders to bury themselves in his thick pelt of hair. The sharp angles and hard planes of his body complimented her delicate curves as she pressed closer, and she reveled in the feel of his strong arms tightening around her as his mouth ravaged hers.

He broke the kiss long before she was ready. She blinked up at him, doing her best to ignore the greedy voice in her head shouting for more. She settled on a lightly teasing tone, and was pleased with the attempt, even if it did come out a little more breathy than she'd planned. "You do that very well, Trevor Bryce."

A muscle twitched along his jaw, and his arms dropped from around her. "You have some talent there yourself, Meggy Calhoun."

What was a woman supposed to say to that? Hell, yeah I do! And why don't you carry me to your bed so we can discover what other talents we both have? She was tempted to say just that. Instead, she took a cleansing breath. "Well."

"Well," he parroted. "Goodnight, Meggy. Sweet dreams."

"You too." She gulped as he disappeared into the night.

## Chapter Six

Meggy heaved an impatient sigh. "It's about time."

Cara and Erin, the youngest O'Shea sister, strolled into Palmer House's kitchen. "Where's Shan?" Erin glanced around the room.

"She'll be down in a minute." Meggy eyed the newspaper in Cara's hand. "Is it in there?"

"Yep."

"Oh, God. Tell me! I can't stand the suspense."

Cara shook her head. "We're waiting for Shan."

"Have you read it?"

"No, I'm waiting for Shan too."

"Then how do you know it's even in there?" Meggy snatched at the paper.

Cara held it out of her reach. "I know because Finn told me. He read it first thing this morning."

"And he didn't tell you what it said?"

"I told him not to." Cara slapped the paper on the table. "We agreed to wait and read any reviews together. We'll wait."

Meggy stomped over to the door leading to the second floor, leaning into the stairwell. "Shannon O'Shea! Don't make me come up there! Your sisters are here with the reviews."

"You're so bossy." Shan's clipped reply competed with the clatter of her feet flying down the steps.

Meggy spun and rushed back to the table to grab the

paper. She scowled when Cara snagged it first then ripped through the pages to the living section.

"Palmer House," she read aloud, "Ambiance and Excellence." When she finished with the glowing review, she looked up at Meggy with a wide grin. "Four stars!"

There was a moment of stunned silence before all hell broke loose. The paper crinkled between them as Meggy grabbed Cara, and Shan and Erin joined the fray. Squealing like little girls at a teen heart-throb sighting, they jumped up and down as one.

Several moments later, the back door swinging open drew Meggy's attention. "Trevor, wait," she called out when he immediately wheeled around to leave. She broke free of the group, scooting around a prep table to grab his arm.

"This definitely feels like a 'girls only' moment." His lips pulled tight in a pained cringe.

She laughed in delight, pulling him further into the room. "We just read our first review." She beamed up at him. "Wallis gave us *four stars*!"

"I saw that. Congratulations." His smile soft, he pulled the folded edition from under his arm and held it out. "I was bringing the paper by. I wasn't sure if you'd seen it yet."

"Oh." She stared at the newspaper in his hand. The way she felt was the oddest thing, like laughing and crying at the same time. She was in the middle of an emotional breakdown, and she didn't care. With a sobbing laugh, she threw herself at him, wrapping her arms around his waist and hugging him fiercely. "Four stars! Can you believe it?"

His arms came around her, and like a cat, she

rubbed her cheek against the softness of his shirt. *God, he smelled good.* Four stars! *And he felt even better.* She burrowed closer, doing her best not to bawl like a baby. She wasn't quite successful. A tortured hiccup escaped.

His hands grasped her shoulders, and he stepped back until he held her at arms' length. Panic filled his eyes. "Oh, shit. Don't. Don't do that!"

"It's just adrenaline." Laughing in spite of the tears dripping down her cheeks, she swiped at them with stiff fingers.

He nodded warily and edged backward toward the door.

Meggy stopped him with a hand on his arm. "Wait, Trevor. You've met Cara." She indicated Cara's sisters. "These are her sisters, Shan and Erin."

He nodded a greeting, looking so endearingly uncomfortable as he continued to inch toward the door that she wanted to grab him once again and bury herself in his arms.

She didn't, and he made his escape with amazing speed.

"It was sweet of you to bring the review by," Erin called out just before the door closed behind him. She pinned Meggy with narrowed eyes. "Well, well."

"Bite me, Erin." She choked on a laugh. She'd known Erin wouldn't let the moment pass, but couldn't bring herself to care. It *had* been sweet that he'd thought to bring her the paper and the review. And the panic in his eyes at her blubbering had been adorable.

There was just something about the man that made her feel all soft and shivery inside. What was a woman supposed to do about that, other than take the next step and see where it led?

"Oh, I know that look." Cara crossed her arms and leaned against the counter.

Meggy turned to find three pairs of identical green eyes watching her with undisguised interest.

"What look?"

"The same look you had when you stole Paul Peterson from Amy Holbrook in high school."

She frowned indignantly. "I didn't steal Paul from Amy. They broke up."

"Only after he got a look at you in that red bikini."

Meggy scowled and propped her hands on her hips. "Now, how exactly was that my fault? I didn't do anything. I was just there. Can I help it Amy showed up in the same suit, and looked like a twelve-year-old boy in it?"

"You're getting off point here, ladies," Shan interrupted. "We were talking about our tenant. The one you just shared a touching embrace with." She turned a stern stare on Meggy "What's going on?"

"Nothing." She shrugged.

"It didn't look like *nothing* to me." Erin cocked her head. "He didn't exactly shove you out of his arms." She hesitated for a heartbeat. "Well, not until he noticed the waterworks." She grinned at Shan. "Did you see his face? It was priceless."

Meggy didn't join her friends in their laughter, but she did smile. "I like him, that's all." Pulling a large bowl from a shelf, she began her dessert preparations. "He's a nice guy."

"He's a nice, gorgeous guy."

She slanted Cara a sly look. "Noticed that, did you?"

"We all did," Shan pointed out. "So, what's going

on between the two of you?"

"Nothing," she repeated, only to be met with three disbelieving stares. With a roll of her eyes, she accepted the inevitable. The O'Shea women were as close to her as sisters, and they knew her well enough to know when she was hedging. They wouldn't be going anywhere until she admitted all. "Okay, fine." She crossed her arms over her chest defiantly. "He kissed me, all right? And I liked it."

"When was this?" Shan shot a quick glance at her sisters. "He just moved in three days ago."

"I couldn't sleep after we closed up last night. He was out back, and so was I. We were just talking, and one thing led to another and..." She broke off, pressing a hand to her belly. "Holy cow! Does that man know how to kiss! I barely stopped myself from ripping his clothes off, and throwing him to the ground."

Shan's eyes widened, and she turned to gape at Cara and Erin. All three burst out laughing.

"I'm taking advantage of being closed on Monday and asking him out. I just have to think of something to do with him." She glowered at Cara's grin. "Besides that!"

Erin was thoughtful for a moment before her eyes brightened. "Ryan has to work Monday night. If he hasn't already given his Celtics tickets to someone else, you can take Trevor to the basketball game." She whipped out her phone and started punching in numbers to call her husband.

"Oh, the man's a goner," Cara predicted. "What guy wouldn't be seduced by floor seats at the Garden?"

"Who said anything about seducing him?" she protested.

"You did." All three sisters spoke as one.

"I did not! Considering ripping his clothes off was a healthy sexual fantasy, not a blueprint for seduction."

"Semantics," Erin quipped over her shoulder, proving she was capable of following more than one conversation at a time. "Love you, baby." She snapped the phone closed. "The tickets are yours if you want them."

Cara studied Meggy's stubborn face. "From the way he was looking at you when you grabbed him, I'd say those tickets will just be overkill."

Erin snickered, and Cara and Shan grinned.

But Meggy just sighed. "I can't believe I'm admitting this to you three busybodies, but I like him. I'm not saying I wouldn't like him naked too." She smiled widely. "But I like him, that's all." She ended with a shrug.

"So what's the problem?" Cara laid a hand on her arm.

"There's no problem. Not really. It's just that..." Reluctant confusion filled her. "Oh, I don't know. It's just that he's not like any other man I've ever met. I think I could *really* like him with a little time, and that scares the crap out of me."

"Suck it up, Calhoun." Cara squeezed her arm and let go. She smiled at her frown. "So you like the guy. If it turns out he's the one for you, there isn't anything you can do about it anyway. You're already a goner." She wrapped an arm around Meggy's shoulders, bumped their hips together and grinned. "Spend some time with him. Get to know him. Better yet, seduce him with the Celtics tickets. You know you want to."

Her smile was slow and thoughtful. The basketball

game *would* be a nice diversion, but she didn't need floor seats to seduce Trevor Bryce. That was something she could do all on her own. And, she thought, she might decide to do just that.

Chapter Seven

By midday Monday, Trevor had to admit there was a good chance he'd been wrong about Meggy Calhoun. The question of whether or not Ashford blood ran through her veins remained, and what she'd been doing at the farm was still a mystery, but he no longer believed her capable of running a con.

With each passing hour, it had become increasingly more difficult to equate the bright, compassionate, quirky woman running the Palmer House kitchen with the money-hungry con artist he'd expected to find when he'd come to town. He'd had no trouble finding locals willing to speak with him about the town and Meggy. Over at the Bluebell Diner, the apparent headquarters for the town grapevine Meggy and Jill had mentioned, gossip was a side dish, served along with the home cooking coming out of the busy kitchen. He'd been back several times for more of both.

On each subsequent visit, he'd been barraged by locals competing to answer his questions. By all accounts, Meggy Calhoun was a pit bull when she put her mind to something, but she wasn't devious. You knew where you stood with the tiny powerhouse, they all insisted, and despite her straightforwardness, or perhaps because of it, the townspeople tended to like her.

Among other things, he'd learned that she and Cara

had been inseparable friends since grade school. After witnessing the easy friendship between the two women, he'd already been forced to discard the idea of the Finnegans being a target of any con she might be pulling.

The possibility of her being partners in crime with the big, blonde bruiser was a dead end as well. According to the report he'd received, Justin Cooper was one of Boston's finest and, by all indications, he was a clean cop.

In truth, nothing he'd seen or learned about her since coming to town indicated Meggy was capable of what he'd been accusing her of in his mind. In fact, just the opposite seemed true. She appeared to be an open, loving, loyal woman, feverishly content with the life she'd carved out for herself.

The question of whether or not she had been adopted by the Calhouns still hadn't been answered. He was tempted to ask her outright, but the tiny seed of doubt that still lingered in his mind had him holding back. His investigator was still digging, and just in case he was totally misreading the situation, because his gonads were clouding his judgment, he'd wait.

Kissing her had been a mistake.

The tangy sweetness of her mouth had haunted him for days. He'd never let lust interfere with a project before, and he couldn't afford to do so now. His grandmother was relying on him. He wouldn't see her hurt, not by anyone.

So where exactly did that leave him? It all kept coming back to her showing up on Martha's Vineyard only to turn around and walk away again. Nearly two weeks later, she hadn't returned to the farm and hadn't made any kind of claim.

And yet, her resemblance to Anne was undeniable. The pictures he'd seen of Anne in her early twenties could have been taken of Meggy this morning. They said everyone had a twin. Could it be just an incredible coincidence after all?

He sprawled back in the oversized chair, and turned his head to glance through the window at Palmer House. Whatever the truth, things were going to get dicey when his true identity was revealed. And it would be soon. Elizabeth's insistence on meeting Meggy at the end of his three weeks would see to that. Even if this situation turned out to be one big coincidence, the damage would be done, and tonight's *date* with the pixie chef was only going to complicate matters.

He'd been surprised when Meggy knocked on his door Saturday afternoon, dressed in her chef's garb, ready for the night ahead. Her smile uncharacteristically shy, she stood shivering in the wind beyond the threshold. No time to come in, she insisted. She'd just dropped by to say she had tickets for Monday night's Celtics game, and would he like to join her?

He should have declined. That would have been the smart thing to do, the honorable thing. The situation was already complicated enough without adding a romantic tangle to the mix, but he hadn't wanted to say no, damn it.

The truth was he wanted the little fairy with her expressive face and trim little body, and he wasn't accustomed to denying himself a woman he wanted. Besides, she'd used the perfect bait with those Celtics tickets. How was a man supposed to resist that kind of double temptation?

As if his musings had summoned her, he heard the tap on the door and rose to answer. She hadn't dressed to dazzle him, yet the faded jeans and oversized, soft, green sweater were still sexy as hell as far as he was concerned. As was the fairy smile lighting her face like a ray of sunshine. There was no denying the sharp pull of desire in his loins, and with an inward shrug, he accepted it was going to be a long night.

"Hi," she greeted softly.

"Hi, yourself." He returned her smile.

"Are you ready for a night of fun and basketball?"

"Are the two mutually exclusive?" His remark was rewarded when she laughed.

"You're a Celts fan?"

"I don't quite qualify for rabid status, but it's a close thing."

"A man after my own heart." She batted her eyes with an exaggerated sigh.

He couldn't resist, didn't want to. Cupping her chin in his hand, he lifted her face and bent until his mouth covered hers. Her lips were soft beneath his and accepting of his caress as he tasted her briefly before lifting his head and stepping back. Enormously pleased at the glazed look in her eyes, he left her standing at the door and crossed the room to grab his keys.

"Ready?" He stopped in front of her and could only grin when she blinked up at him, mumbled something about secret weapons, and spun on her heel to lead him out to the parking lot.

\*\*\*\*

Meggy had made reservations at a little Italian place in the North End of Boston, within walking distance of the Boston Garden. Linking her arm through Trevor's, they strolled the cobbled bricks of Boston's oldest neighborhood.

The narrow streets were teaming with pedestrian traffic as the city's workforce called it a day, swarming the dining district for an early dinner before heading home or to the game. It amused her to see the many female glances aimed Trevor's way because really, she couldn't blame the women for looking.

His dark auburn hair gleamed like a thick pelt in the fading afternoon light, and his swarthy skin gave him a healthy glow. Understated wealth oozed from every pore of his lanky body, which showcased the natural-colored, Irish woolen sweater and faded jeans as perfectly as it had the expensive business-suit.

The man was a clotheshorse, she thought with a grin. Even his play clothes looked as if they'd been tailored to fit him to perfection. Not that she was complaining. When he'd opened the carriage house door at her knock, she'd had to fight back the urge to lick her lips and jump him. She'd settled for a sigh, a silent one, or so she'd thought. Had he heard the yearning in that breathy little huff? Had that been the reason he'd grabbed her and without a word, kissed her senseless?

The knowing humor in his pale eyes when he finally set her back on her feet told her he'd had a fairly good idea of the direction in which her mind had wandered. His cocky smile confirmed it. Oh, yeah, Trevor Bryce was dangerous.

They were seated immediately at a booth near the window, and when the waiter came for their orders, she suggested the manicotti. The busy, family-owned restaurant was one of her favorites and had the best manicotti west of Italy, she promised.

He bowed to her expertise, and when he groaned in appreciation at his first bite, her smile was smug. "You're a regular here?" Trevor's fork stilled before he dived into his dessert.

"I'm a regular wherever there's delicious food *I* don't have to cook." She grinned. "I haunt several spots around the North End. I've stolen some of my favorite recipes within a half mile of here."

"Meggy Calhoun, culinary crook."

*Well, look at him. He's even sexy when he teases.* Delighted at the description, she laughed. "You could call it that, but I only keep the recipes for my personal use. I work too hard on my own to take credit for someone else's."

"You love being a chef." It was a statement more than a question.

"It's all I've ever wanted."

"You never wanted to do anything else?"

"Not for as long as I can remember." She cocked her head. "Unless you count the few minutes I considered joining the circus when I was nine. I was dazzled by a lady juggler in a sequined body-suit." Crinkles appeared at the corners of his pale eyes when he grinned, and she thought the laugh lines only made him more appealing. "It took me less than five minutes to decide that getting to wear one of those fantastic, sparkly costumes wouldn't be worth putting up with the smell of the elephants."

"I don't know," his voice dropped to a rumbling drawl. "I think it would be worth holding my breath for a while for the chance to see you in a sequined body-costume."

A tiny shiver of pleasure raced through her system

at his words and tone. "Well, you're out of luck," she said cheekily. "Turns out I can't juggle."

"Isn't that always the way?" He shook his head with mock disappointment.

"What about you?" She propped her elbows on the table, studying him. "What did you want to be when you were growing up?"

"I always knew I would go into the family business. Finance, real estate, but I did have a secret dream of being a pirate for a while."

"A pirate?" She laughed. "What century were you born in?"

The grin he shot her was wide. "Hey, I was six, and my father had just taken me to see the tall ships."

"Well, then, that's okay. Cara and I came into town a couple of years ago when the tall ships were in the harbor. They're pretty impressive."

"They're even more impressive from on board." He stopped eating for a minute, his eyes taking on a dreamy quality. "I had the opportunity to sail on one a couple of years later during the parade of ships around New York Harbor." Dark brows waggled, and leaning in, he curved his lips in a buccaneer's leer. "A pirate's dream come true."

"Wow." She blinked with exaggerated innocence. "Or should I say, 'Aaargh'?" That warm and mushy sensation returned to her belly when he threw back his head on a laugh. "So, what happened to the dream? Why didn't you go to sea and become the scourge of the Atlantic?"

He sat back, his smile wry. "Seasickness."

Her eyes widened. "You got seasick on a tall ship?"

"No, I did fine there. A deep sea fishing adventure

with twenty foot swells killed my desire for a seafaring life. I love to sail, though. In fact, I have my own cruiser. I just don't get out on the water as much as I'd like these days."

Their waiter stopped at the table to ask if they needed anything else. Alone once again, he touched the tip of her finger with his, sending her hormonal system into overload. "Have you always lived in Palmerton?"

She nodded. "Except for the year and a half I studied in Paris. My parents were both born in Palmerton. They moved to Maine when they retired." She smiled happily. "My dad was a teacher, and my mom worked at the nursery on the edge of town. You should talk to them. They could help you with your research."

****

He planned to. There were a number of questions he'd like to put to Bob and Carol Calhoun, not the least of which being whether or not Meggy was their natural child. "You're close to them?"

She looked at him strangely, as if the question made no sense.

"Of course. They're my parents."

"Not everyone is close to their family."

She nodded, cocking her head as she considered him. "Were you? I know your father passed away when you were young. What about your mother?"

"She died when I was five."

A stricken expression flashed in her eyes, and she reached across the table to cover his hand with hers. "Oh, God."

He stared at her hand. With its tapered fingers and clear-polished nails, it looked incredibly delicate over his much larger one. Automatically, he turned his own hand over until hers rested in his grasp, palm to palm. Meeting her gaze, he shook his head at the compassionate empathy in her crystal blue eyes. "It's not quite the tragedy it sounds. I miss them, but I had a good childhood."

"But you were an orphan. Who raised you?"

Her voice was sad, which touched something deep in his soul. "My grandmother."

"You were close?"

"We still are. She's a tough old girl, but she has a heart as big as they come."

"You love her." Her pixy face beamed a soft smile. "That's nice."

The irony of the situation didn't escape him. If Meggy was who Elizabeth believed her to be, he was sitting here becoming more and more intrigued by a woman who had more right to his grandmother's love and protection than he ever had. Despite warning himself against letting it happen, he had become fascinated by a woman he'd set out to destroy. A woman he found himself wanting until he couldn't think straight. What a mess. "She's my family," he said finally.

And possibly yours. He hoped she'd take his love for Elizabeth into consideration once she learned the truth.

Chapter Eight

The corridors of Boston Garden were crowded with fans, waiting in long lines at the many concession stands or moving toward the tunneled openings to find their seats. Trevor stopped to purchase a beer for each of them while Meggy propped herself against the wall close by to people watch. When he rejoined her, and handed her a large cup full of golden brew, she could only shake her head. "We just finished eating." She eyed the hot dog and large popcorn he carried. "Are you still hungry?"

"I'm always hungry." He shook his head in resignation. "Quick metabolism. But, the hot dog isn't strictly for my stomach."

"Excuse me?"

His shoulders moved in an accepting shrug. "It's tradition. The last time I caught a game and didn't have one, the Celts were blown out by the Magic." He frowned. "I won't make *that* mistake again."

She stared wide-eyed. "I'd say you're a bit closer to rabid than you want to admit."

His pale eyes sparkled. "Did I mention I bleed green?"

That made her laugh. She jerked her head in a *follow me* motion. "Come on, Roger Rabid. I promised you a treat."

He flipped over the floor seats, and they spent the

next three hours cheering on the boys in green to a home town victory. Driving home through the night, they discussed the current roster and argued over possible off-season trades and the draft. They agreed on, and hoped for, the possibility of another title this season.

"I had fun tonight," she said as he pulled to a stop in the Palmer House parking lot. Quiet descended on the interior of the vehicle when he switched off the ignition.

"So did I." He brushed the curve of her cheek with the tip of one long finger. "It's early yet. Would you like to come over to the carriage house? I've got a nice bottle of wine in the fridge."

Pleasure coursed through her at the idea of continuing the evening and at the unspoken question in his eyes. It seemed too fast to be feeling what she was for this man, and yet she'd expected this was where they were heading from the moment she'd first placed her hand in his.

Jumping into bed with every man she shared an evening with wasn't her habit, but she wasn't exactly a blushing virgin either. Her experience wasn't vast, and she'd dated both men for weeks before she'd finally gone to bed with them. Still, what she'd felt for those other men held no resemblance to what she'd been feeling from the moment she'd clapped eyes on Trevor Bryce.

She sighed. Ultimately, whether it happened tonight, or in a week, or even a month, she knew they'd eventually become intimate. The pull between them was too strong to resist. With Trevor, she found she didn't want to resist what he made her feel. She wanted to experience the act of making love, when love was actually part of the act.

Her heart did a fast, spiraling roll in her chest. No, that wasn't right. She didn't fool herself into believing she was in love with him. She wasn't. But she could be with a little time. The possibility should scare the crap out of her, but she found she didn't want to pass up the opportunity to take the next step and see where it led.

You've lost your mind, Calhoun, the voice in her head warned, and she couldn't help but agree. With a mental shrug for the loss of her sanity, she looked him straight in the eye, and embraced her own madness. "Are you inviting me to your bed, Trevor?"

His fingertip grazed over her bottom lip. His pale gaze burned. "I believe that's exactly what I'm doing."

In the close darkness of the car, she nodded and leaned across the console to press her lips to his before opening the door to climb out. She waited while he skirted the hood, and when he held out his hand, she folded her fingers with his.

He led her to the carriage house door, flipping the switch just inside and flooding the apartment with light. "Are you sure about this, Meggy?" His gaze bore into hers. "Because once I close this door, there won't be any going back, for either of us."

Her answer was to step into his arms.

His head lowered until their lips meshed, and she felt him reach out blindly to push the door closed behind her. The blast of heat that ripped through her at that first touch of mouth on mouth seared away any shyness she expected to experience with this, their first time together. Though they were new, the sensations and textures of the pleasures assailing her were somehow familiar, as though he'd touched her just there, pressed against her that way, and kissed her like that, a thousand times before.

She rose on her toes, pressing closer, and her moan matched his at the full body contact. One large hand dropped to her bottom. Her feet left the floor. Her head spun. She clung to him, burying her hands in his hair and wrapping her legs around his trim waist.

"From the first time you turned your fairy smile on me," his deep voice rumbled, "I've wanted to bite this spot. Here." He bit down gently on her full lower lip. "Right, here." With his tongue, he soothed the nip.

Her laugh was throaty and ended on a dizzy squeak when he moved suddenly, spinning with her clamped to him by a muscled arm below her bottom. With long strides, he crossed the room and lowered her to the bed.

"I don't have a fairy smile." Humor was full in her denial as he followed her down to cover her body with his own.

Braced on one arm, he leaned over her and traced her lips with a callused fingertip. "Baby, I half expected you to start casting fae spells the first time you smiled at me."

Delighted laughter escaped her at his whimsy, and he covered her mouth with his, capturing it. "You taste like sunshine," he murmured.

*He* was the one casting spells. What else would explain this sudden leaping of every nerve ending in her body? She felt as though she were floating, even as she shimmered with pleasure at the weight of his big body pressing her into the coverlet beneath her.

The brush of his fingers left gooseflesh behind as his fingertips skimmed the tender flesh of her throat, continuing down over the soft material of her sweater. They paused at the tightened peak of one breast, those talented fingers circling the hardened nub through the layers of cloth. And then he was cupping her, his large hand measuring the generous mound. She was helpless against the shock of sensation and arched her back to increase the contact.

Her mind was already dazed with pleasure when his mouth left hers.

He pulled back to look down into her half-closed eyes. "I want to look at you." He slipped his hand beneath the hem of her sweater. She nodded and his hand moved upward, baring her belly to his view.

She caught a flash of molten silver as his desire-darkened eyes followed the movement of his hand.

Then he leaned down to nibble at her bare middle.

The delicate skin at her navel quivered at the contact with his testing tongue. His laugh was dark at her involuntary response.

Brushing his cheek against her sensitive skin, he turned his head to look up at her. A stormy gray-eyed gaze met hers. "Let me see you, Meggy."

In silent consent, she reached for the hem of her sweater. His hands joined hers to help strip it away. She shifted her shoulders to aide in its removal, laughing at the sight of the green wool sailing through the air when he tossed it aside. A smile remained on her face, even as she reveled at the sight of his gaze growing even darker as they roamed over her.

"For such a tiny little thing…" He brushed his fingertips along the swell above her lacy bra, "you're well blessed here. So soft," he whispered, caressing the quivering mounds.

"Trevor," she breathed.

"What is it you want, little fairy?" He curled the tip

of a finger under the lace. "This?" He rubbed at the straining tip.

The word she spoke was both plea and moan. "Please."

He tugged at the strip of sheer lace until a turgid nipple popped free. The stab of his tongue against the tightened bud made her back arch up off the bed, her arms coming down to capture his head. She moaned at the pull of his mouth on her as though he meant to swallow her whole.

The front clasp of her bra snapped free without her notice, and his mouth moved to her other breast, treating it to the same loving attention. With mouth and fingers, he worshiped the bountifulness of her until she felt her own blood thicken within her like warmed honey. A whimper escaped her lips at the loss of sensation when he lifted his head, even as her frantic fingers jerked at the sweater covering his chest, desperate for the feel of heated flesh.

He sat up to strip the offending garment over his head, and the sight of all that dusky, sculpted skin had her scrambling up onto her knees.

"What's good for the goose..." Greedily, she pressed her palms to the muscled planes of his chest. Like a blind woman, she learned his form, palms savoring, brushing at the light dusting of springy hair here, fingers testing, pressing into pads of muscle there. "God, you're gorgeous."

She spread her hands over the wide expanse of warm skin and couldn't stop herself from leaning in to press a kiss to the skin over his heart. Her questing fingers found one tiny nipple in the dark spray of hair, and she licked at it like a kitten, humming her pleasure.

His low groan of response thrilled and delighted her.

With a grin, she straightened. She sat back on her heels and met his heated gaze. "I'm still wearing my boots."

"You have entirely too much on." A big hand to her chest sent her sprawling onto her back. Her laughter pealed through the quiet apartment as he went about addressing the situation. Stripping her of her boots and jeans, he fingered her lacy panties. "I approve of your choice of underwear, baby." He pressed a kiss to the lacy green material covering her. "But these need to go."

Dizzy with anticipation, she fingered the button of his jeans. "They go when these go."

With an urgency that had her laughter returning, he jackknifed until he was flat on his back. He shed himself of his own boots and jeans with more motion than grace, and then rolled to his side to look down at her once more. Sliding his fingers down her flat belly, he slipped the lacy panties down her legs until she lay naked under his hot gaze. "So much in such a little package." His eyes were the color of a turbulent winter storm when they met hers. "You're beautiful, Meggy."

"When you look at me like that, I *feel* beautiful," she admitted artlessly.

His mouth covered hers in a searing kiss, and she lost herself to the feel of her lover's hands on her. He explored her textures with gentle strokes, touching her everywhere until she was writhing with need beneath his talented exploration.

When a long finger plunged inside her, his groan was low and ragged, and she felt herself slipping toward explosion. Frantic, her fingers clawed at his briefs, shoving them down his hips to be kicked aside.

"Inside you, Meggy." His voice was a guttural growl. "I need to be inside you."

Heartily agreeing, she could only nod. She watched him cover himself with a condom from a packet waiting on the bedside table.

Then he mounted her, seating himself between her thighs.

Molten silver smoldered down at her from his darkened eyes.

"Watch me while I make you mine, fairy girl." And with an utterly male smile, he slid inside her.

The feeling of coming home left her shattered and wholly unable to control the frantic race toward paradise. His stormy gaze held her captive, and she eagerly followed him when he began to move into unspeakable pleasure.

She tried to hold back the looming completion, wanting to savor this first time, joined completely with him, but it was hopeless. Her muscles tensed, and she called out to him blindly as she imploded, shattering into a million flaming pieces to swirl aimlessly on the winds of ecstasy. She was nearly deaf to his triumphant cry as he joined her there.

## Chapter Nine

Moments passed, or perhaps it was hours. She wasn't sure. He was heavy. Not that it mattered. There was no way she could move, even if she'd wanted to.

"Sorry. I must be crushing you."

The only sound she could manage was a purr.

Male satisfaction vibrated through her with his chuckle. "Meggy?" She opened her eyes, and though he wore a sated smile, concern softened his eyes. "Am I too heavy for you?"

"Not too heavy." She gave a contented sigh. "You make a nice blanket."

His eyes sparkled with humor, and he pressed a soft kiss to her lips. She felt a twinge of regret when he disengaged their still-joined bodies. He grabbed the corner of the quilt to flick it over her nude body. For the first time, she was aware of the chilliness of the air, and she shivered. Neither of them had noticed the coolness of the apartment when they'd arrived. Need had its own temperature, and it was hot.

Naked, he rose and disappeared inside the tiny bathroom. When he emerged several moments later, she watched him move to the fireplace to flip a switch. Warm and cozy flames leapt to life in the grate, and she decided right then and there the expense of converting the traditional old hearth to gas had been money well spent. Then he turned.

Holy cow! With a gulp, she nearly shouted the words. And who would blame her if she had? What woman could keep her head when treated to the full impact of a very large, and very naked, Trevor Bryce?

She'd been right that first day. Trevor Bryce looked like a Greek god. The swarthy tone of his skin gleamed like teakwood in the flickering light of the fire. His shoulders were broad, and those ripped biceps she'd noted days ago weren't the only proof he kept himself in shape. Six-pack abs and sculpted thighs, nearly as thick as her waist, were a pretty good indication he didn't spend all his time at the computer writing, or following the stock market.

Just looking at him set her heart to racing, as though she hadn't been flattened by that unprecedented orgasm only moments earlier. Her hungry gaze dropped to that most male part of him and widened to see that her admiring contemplation had had a tangible effect on his body. Her guilty gaze flew to his. Simmering interest lay beneath the humor she found there. She blushed at having been caught staring.

"Hold that thought." With a soft chuckle, he winked. "I promised you wine."

Naked, he padded barefoot into the kitchen and rummaged.

She watched, amused, as he glanced around, his arms full. He pulled a decorative basket from the counter. The dried flowers it held were dumped on the table, to be replaced with the items he'd gathered for their late night snack.

He should have looked ridiculous, this big, naked, Wall Street pirate, striding across the apartment with a basket full of edible odds and ends in one hand, and a bottle of wine and two glasses in the other. But the sight didn't make her laugh. It made her mouth water.

He placed the basket on the bed and settled himself beside her.

Propped against the headboard with the quilt tucked modestly beneath her arms, she peered into the basket. "A picnic?" She plucked out a bunch of fat, green grapes.

He leaned over to kiss her, then settled back to pull the cork from the bottle. He poured a glass of wine and handed it to her. "A naked picnic." He spared her a wicked grin.

Her hands full of wine and grapes, she was helpless to prevent him from crooking a finger under the edge of the quilt.

With a tug, he exposed her breasts to his fervent gaze. "A new favorite pastime of mine."

She met his grin with one of her own. Sipping at the glass of chilled, sweet wine, she considered him. "Any pastime involving food seems to be a favorite of yours."

"Pretty much." He pulled items from the basket. "But in this case, it's not just my naturally quick metabolism at work." He looked up from the basket and winked. "A man needs to keep up his strength when he has a sexy fairy in his bed."

She plucked a fat grape from the bunch and popped it into her mouth. Her eyes twinkled with mischief. "Aw, poor baby. Do you need me to whip up a virility potion?"

He glanced down at his lap. "Nope. Doesn't look like that will be necessary." The heat of a blush spread across her cheekbones, and he laughed. "Dig in, fairy girl. I'm not the only one who will need to keep up their strength tonight."

Grinning despite the blush, she reached in the basket and pulled out a yellow box. Her brows snapped together. "You've got to be kidding."

He looked confused. "What? You don't like cheese?"

"That"—she set the box aside to dig in the basket again—"is not cheese. That's a processed, orange lump of...something. But it's not cheese."

He grabbed the box and plucked off the top, peeling back the inner foil to squeeze off a chunk of orange lump. It and the cracker in his hand went into his mouth, and he spoke around the bite. "Leave it to a chef to be a food snob."

Insulted, she paused in the act of opening a jar of pickles to stare at him. "I'm not a food snob. I just don't consider that food."

He snagged a pickle out of the jar in her hands, using it to point at the offending box. "That shit makes the best grilled-cheese sandwiches. In my college years, I lived on that, bread, and beer."

"In my college years, *I* lived on perfectly prepared French cuisine." Nose in the air, she grinned smugly.

He shoved the rest of his pickle into her mouth. "Like I said, food snob."

They shared the wine, nibbling on the food he'd gathered, and each other, until the combined result of the many caresses and kisses had him shoving aside the basket and its contents for more tempting fare. When she slipped into sleep sometime later, surrounded by his warmth, her last thought was that she'd never look at a picnic the same way again.

**\*\*\*\***

Trevor smiled at her murmured sigh as her breathing slowed and evened out. He tucked her more tightly to his side. Though he was tired, his muscles pleasantly wrecked and completely sated from his recent orgasms, his mind was too troubled to allow him to sleep.

He wasn't a man who suffered from indecision. Blessed with the drive to take on the problems of life without hesitation and the intelligence to solve them, he hadn't had a lot of experience with the phenomenon. But the entire situation surrounding Meggy had demolished his usual instincts.

He couldn't have made a bigger mess of things if he'd tried. Whatever Meggy had been doing at the farm, he was ninety-nine percent sure it hadn't been illicit in nature. Not that it mattered now. Whether it turned out she was Rachel's daughter, or simply an innocent woman with a remarkable resemblance to Anne, she was going to be royally pissed when she discovered the truth behind his arrival in Palmerton.

*And if it turns out she's the con artist you thought her to be after all?* The annoyingly suspicious voice in his head chose that moment to be heard from again. He sighed. It no longer mattered which of those possibilities ended up being the truth. He was in trouble regardless.

Staring into the stunned glaze of Meggy's blue eyes as she'd flown apart beneath him, his mind had been full of a single, stark truth; *Meggy Calhoun, whoever, whatever you might be, you're mine.*

It was a hell of a shock when a man realized that, after years of avoiding the emotion, he had finally fallen in love with a woman. When the woman was one he'd been trying to destroy the result was disaster. And that was exactly the position in which he now found himself.

His usually fertile mind cast frantically about for a solution. At thirty-three, he'd had his share of relationships with women, but he'd never loved any of them. He'd be dammed if he'd lose Meggy now that he'd finally found her.

If they'd met under different circumstances, he would have gone after her with every weapon in his arsenal, and he'd have gotten her, too, by God. He'd have gotten her because he wouldn't have let off the pressure until she waved the white flag. He could do no less now.

She had feelings for him. Oh, she may not love him, yet, but she had feelings. She cared. The question was did she care enough to understand and give him the chance to explain the situation when she finally learned the truth? She would if she loved him, his heart insisted.

The key was to make sure her feelings had grown from caring to love before the truth came to light. His odds of soothing her hurt and anger would be much better if she'd already admitted to him, and to herself, that she was his.

With her warm body tucked close to his in the dark, he grinned as several ideas formed on how to expedite his courtship of Meggy Calhoun. He had less than a week to do damage control before Elizabeth demanded a meeting. He'd see Meggy wave that flag first.

Chapter Ten

Meggy emerged from her shower to find all three of the O'Shea sisters sipping coffee at her tiny kitchen table. Without a word, she pulled a mug from the cabinet and poured herself a cup. She sat at the table, sighing in appreciation of her first sip of the strong brew.

"Well?" Erin broke the silence.

"Well, what?"

"What happened on your date?" One of Erin's finely plucked eyebrows quirked.

"Oh, that." She yawned. "We had manicotti at Giordanos, and then we went to the game. Awesome seats, by the way. But if I were you, I'd keep an eye on Ryan. Trevor may try to steal him away."

Erin gaped at her. "He's gay?"

"No, but for those seats he may consider a lifestyle change." She kept a straight face.

"Ha ha," Erin growled as Cara and Shan snickered. "Very funny."

She laughed. "I'm only half kidding. He flipped when he saw where we were sitting. I think he's an even bigger Celts nut than I am."

"That's nice," Shan interrupted, her curiosity no less than Erin's. "Now tell us why I saw you crossing the lawn from the carriage house at six-thirty this morning."

"Oh," Erin squealed, "I knew it! But it's completely

understandable. God, he's so hot, and just a little bit dangerous, don't you think?"

He was dangerous, all right—dangerously sexy.

Cara, who had remained silent up until now, leaned her elbows on the table. "Are you okay?"

Meggy met her worried gaze. "I spent an incredible night with a gorgeous, charming guy. Why wouldn't I be okay?"

Cara sat back, crossing her arms over her chest. She gave her a level look. "You may be the dating queen of Palmerton, but you don't sleep around. And you've *never* slept with a man you've only known for a week."

Despite the three attentive green gazes boring into hers, she remained stubbornly silent for a full ten seconds. Finally, she caved, as they'd known she would. Her cheeks puffed out, and she blew a mystified breath. "I just couldn't help myself."

Shan and Cara snorted with laughter, and Erin stared wide-eyed.

"Well, it's true. I have no willpower where Trevor Bryce is concerned." Contentment was heavy in her sigh. "But, I'm more than okay."

"Details," Erin demanded from across the table. "We want details."

"I don't kiss and tell." She sipped at her coffee.

"Since when?"

Meggy narrowed her eyes at Cara, but then sighed. "Since Trevor, I guess." A glance around the table had her shrugging. "It's different when you realize the guy could be the one."

"Told you." Erin wore a smug expression as she jabbed Shan with an elbow.

"I didn't say he *was* the one, just that he *could* be."

Erin lifted a brow.

"You're pretty calm about this." Cara studied her face.

She leaned her elbows on the table, cradling the mug in her hands. "I know. It's weird, isn't it?" She shook her head in wonder. "I always figured when I finally found a guy I could love, I'd be so freaked out, I'd be off and running in the opposite direction. I *should* be running. I have plans for my life, and falling in love will just screw them up...even if he does look incredible naked."

"*Especially* if he looks incredible naked." Shan slowly nodded, her eyes twinkling.

"Exactly. But I don't feel like running. Just the opposite." She sighed. "I've been steaming along through life for twenty six years without any real wrinkles. Now all of a sudden, I'm dealing with Palmer House opening, the Elizabeth Ashford issue looming, and what do I do? I go and throw myself into a relationship that could change my life. I should be half-crazy with panic, but instead, I feel happy, and excited, and peaceful all at once, you know?"

"Oh, you've got it bad." Erin sprawled back in her chair with a wide smile.

"I do, don't I?" Her lips curled in a serene smile, remembering the hours she'd spent in Trevor's bed. All long-muscled perfection and heat, he'd surprised her with his teasing gentleness.

"What about him?" Cara stilled the movement with a hand to her arm as she brought the coffee mug to her lips again. "How does he feel?"

"I have no idea," she confessed, and then she laughed. "He's taking me sailing this morning."

"Sailing?" Shan and Erin exclaimed together.

"Sailing. He's got his own boat, though I don't think we'll be sailing on it today. I'm not sure where he keeps it." Her brow wrinkled in thought. "Come to think of it, I'm not exactly sure where he lives."

"See," Cara sat back in her chair, "that's the trouble with guys with cute butts. You forget to ask the pertinent questions, like do you live in this hemisphere?"

She smirked at Cara's innocent look, ignoring Shan's and Erin's chuckles. "Who was it that took one look at Finn's ass and couldn't dredge up the slightest interest in another male from then on?"

"Touché." Cara grinned.

"Anyway, I may not know exactly where he lives, but I did ask. He works up and down the east coast. He said he has a place in Virginia, but he spends a lot of time in Boston and Atlanta. He's got money that his father left him when he died, and he apparently invested it well. So, he's not some deadbeat after me for my money. Which is a good thing, since I'm technically broke."

"We could always hire an investigator," Cara offered. "Have him checked out."

The suggestion horrified her. "No, I don't want to do that. I would hate it if someone was sneaking around behind my back like that. Besides, he just signed a six-month lease, so we'll have plenty of time to get to know one another. All I know is he makes me feel all soft and mushy inside, and I don't seem to be able to do a damn thing about that. The only option I see is convincing him he feels the same way."

"Amen, sister," Erin piped in, and they all laughed.

That had been her strategy with Ryan, and she'd succeeded wonderfully.

Meggy sighed, remembering the look in his smoky eyes as he'd slipped inside her. "If I'm reading him right, he's halfway there already. So, we'll take it slow. Well, not too slow." She wiggled her brows. "I plan to enjoy myself while deciding what I want to do with him. If I decide to keep him, I'll just have to see to it he says the words first." Confidence warred with insecurity, and thankfully, confidence won the fight.

Cara laughed, and tapped her mug against hers. Shan and Erin followed suit. "To keepers!" Cara toasted. She waited until Meggy brought the mug to her lips to add, "So, did you take any pictures?"

\*\*\*\*

Trevor's big Mercedes was luxurious, the ride smooth. When he stopped in front of the Bluebell Diner, Meggy raised her brows in question.

"Tess promised to pack us a bagged lunch. I just need to run in and pick it up." He pressed a quick kiss to her lips then slid from the car.

She stared after him as he disappeared inside the diner. Tess? He'd been in town less than a week, and he was already on a first-name basis with the Bluebell's pretty waitress? Hmmm.

"Tess?" she asked the moment he settled himself back behind the wheel with a large paper sack. "Didn't take you long to get friendly with the locals, did it?"

He grinned and handed her their lunch. "Just doing research, fairy girl. The Bluebell is a great source for those yarns you told me about. I've met several of the town's more colorful and more talkative citizens while bellied up to the counter, including Maive Cataldo and

Jasper Watson."

The flash of jealousy she'd felt at the thought of Trevor spending time with the pretty Tess cooled at the mention of the town's two oldest citizens. She smiled. "Maive keeps everyone in line at the Bluebell, but Jasper is an old sweetheart, isn't he?"

Trevor eased the big car out onto the road. "'Sweetheart' isn't a word I'd use to describe the old goat, but I know what you mean. He's a character."

She chuckled. "He's an institution in Palmerton and a hopeless flirt. He's proposed to every woman in town at one time or another. His wife, Bertie, is a saint."

"Her name has come up a couple of times."

"You should make a point of talking to her. She's led a pretty interesting life. Did you know she was a welder down at the shipyards before Jasper came back from the war? A real life Rosie the Riveter. And Jasper's sister Clara was a naval nurse. She's a hoot."

"And wears some interesting hats." Trevor laughed.

"You *have* been busy." She eyed him, not really surprised he'd already met so many of the townsfolk. He was here to do research, after all. She was interested to hear what he thought of Clara, though. Like her brother, ninety-three-year old Clara Watson was a fixture around town, and didn't go anywhere without a hat. She had long been the reigning queen of eccentricity in Palmerton. "So, you've met our Clara."

"I had lunch with her at the Bluebell on Sunday," he explained with an indulgent smile. "She insisted on going Dutch, and then paid her half with five empty gum wrappers."

"That sounds like Clara."

"She had a brown paper bag folded up like a clutch

purse. It was decorated with crayons and glitter to match the paper flowers glued to her straw hat."

"Hard to believe she's the richest woman in town, isn't it?" His stunned expression made her laugh out loud. "Their family once owned the mineral rights to a large chunk of the North Shore. You have something in common with the Watsons, Trevor. Jasper and Clara made some very wise investments when they sold the rights."

He stared at her open-mouthed for a long moment. Then his jaw snapped shut with an audible click. "I've been *had* by a pair of geriatric swindlers," he grumbled, shaking his head. "I've picked up both of their tabs at the Bluebell for the last three days."

Meggy burst into uncontrollable laughter.

He frowned. "You think that's funny, do you?"

"Oh, Trevor, you've been had by more than just a couple of crafty old-timers."

"How so?"

She controlled her mirth long enough to inform him. "The Watsons *own* the Bluebell."

Again, he was silent, studying her face for the truth. Wry acceptance was heavy in his sigh. "I'm losing my touch. I used to be able to read people. No one in this town is who they appear to be."

"Cheer up, Trevor." She patted his arm in sympathy. "They've spent ninety plus years perfecting their acts. It took you less than a week to catch on. Cara's dad bought Jasper breakfast for two months when they first moved to town. They've been conning newcomers since the diner opened."

She grinned when he glanced at her sharply.

"Don't be surprised to find an envelope full of cash

shoved at you once you let it be known you're on to them. They're not cheap. They just have a running contest to see who can run up the biggest tab. The next time you're in there, ask one of them about the pair of ceramic cows up above the cash register. That's where they keep their ill-gotten gains."

Trevor shook his head in disbelief. "Small towns."

"You have no idea. But there's no surer way of knowing you've been accepted in Palmerton than to have your cash in those cows. The Watsons don't waste their talent on people they don't like. Clara especially, she's a very discriminating woman."

"Yeah, I could tell that by her paper purse," he grumbled.

She giggled. The man was so darned sexy when he grumbled. "I didn't say she isn't eccentric, just a good judge of character. So, you've discovered the Bluebell. How is your research coming along? And the book? Can I read what you have so far?"

"No." He kept his gaze focused on the road.

"Come on, Trevor," she wheedled. "I've never tried to write anything, but I'm sure I could be a big help with your story. I have a vivid imagination."

"And I've never tried to cook, but I have an insatiable appetite. Shall I come help you in the Palmer House kitchen?"

"Not on your life."

One corner of his lips lifted in a smug smile, but then, her smile was smug as well.

Chapter Eleven

They crossed into Boston on the Tobin Bridge, exiting the highway, heading into Charlestown. Trevor wove his way through the narrow streets to the marina parking lot. The gleaming masts and blinding white hulls of the docked vessels painted a perfect picture against the dark water of the harbor. They climbed from the car.

The occasional screech of seagulls and dull gong of buoys disturbed the soothing lap of water against docked hulls. The cool, yet humid, breeze carried the sharp tang of the sea and the intermittent waft of cooking food from the many restaurants across the harbor. She snapped pictures while Trevor carried their lunch.

Over the wooden planks of the dock, they made their way past the impressive yachts berthed on either side. Her eyes widened as she gaped at the sleek, white sailboat when he stopped. Noting the name emblazoned in bold, golden letters on the stern, she looked up at him. "Christos' Chariot?"

"Christos is a family name." He passed her the bagged lunch and handed her aboard. "And she's well named. She rides the wind." He invited her to look around, leaving her to her own devices as he went about preparing to sail.

She knew nothing about sailing, or sailboats for that matter, but she knew expensive when she saw it. The forty-foot cruiser gleamed in the morning sunlight. Trimmed in glossy teak, she slid a hand over the smooth surface of the wood, admiring the craftsmanship while avoiding the intimidating rigging. "Do you need me to help with the ropes, or sails, or anything?" she called from where she stood at the rail. "Can you drive this thing without anyone to help? It seems awfully complicated."

He laughed and continued preparing to shove off. "I can sail her on my own. You just sit back and enjoy the ride today. You can play first mate another time."

*Another time. Oh, I like the sound of that.* With a smile, she continued along the deck. She admired the large lounging couch formed into the deck along the front bow, then wandered back to the partially enclosed bridge with its impressive controls and captain's chair. Shading her eyes with one hand, she pressed her nose to the smoked glass doors leading to below deck.

"Would you like a tour before we shove off?" Trevor appeared beside her.

"Do we have enough time?" She turned and smiled. "This thing is huge."

His head dropped to hers to press a quick kiss to her mouth before he slid the door open. At the bottom of four laddered steps was a large galley. On the left, the port side, he explained, was a table and built-in L-shaped bench. On the right, the starboard, a gleaming white, U-shaped counter included a four burner stove and oven, stainless steel sink, and a glossy black refrigerator-freezer. On both sides of the galley, clean-lined windows followed the shape of the hull and let in the scenery.

She turned slowly. "All the conveniences of home."

He grinned and took her hand, pushing open a set of louvered doors.

She leaned to look down the companionway at the comfortable-looking double bed framed in the shape of the hull.

"Guest berth," he explained before leading her back around the main stairs. He paused at a door, opening it. "The head."

She glanced around him at the full bathroom, complete with a generously sized shower enclosure.

He tugged her toward the back of the boat until he came to another door. He swung it open and stood to the side. A king-sized bed took up much of the large cabin, but the room was far from crowded with its built-in, teak-wood cabinetry, writing desk, and book shelves. The bed looked spacious and inviting with a masculine flair, done up in shades of burgundy and cream.

"Very nice." She stepped inside to investigate. "There's a lot more room here than you would think."

"The builder is known for his clever use of space. He's utilized every square inch, which translates into comfort and convenience, as well as efficiency."

"And charm." She ran her hand along the smooth wood of the desk. "It's beautiful. Is yours like this?"

"Mine?"

"Your boat."

His brows were arched when she glanced his way over one shoulder.

"*Just* like this." He smiled gently. "This is my boat."

She straightened from studying the bindings on a shelf of books. Slowly, she turned to face him. "This is yours?"

"Whose did you think she was?" Humor danced in his eyes.

"I don't know. I just thought..." She shrugged. "I thought you'd rented it, or borrowed it, or something." Her head cocked in thought. "You keep your boat docked in Charlestown? I thought you lived in Virginia."

"I live in your carriage house at the moment. I just signed a six-month lease, remember?"

"Well, yes. But..."

"I had her brought up here so she would be available if and when I found the time to sail."

"Oh."

He took the step necessary to reach her and lifted her chin in his palm until her eyes met his. "Is there a problem, Meggy?"

"No," she said softly. "No, I just didn't realize..." His? This three-dimensional billboard for incredible wealth was his? The conversation with the girls flitted through her mind. She really *didn't* know him. She was well on her way to falling in love with a man she knew next to nothing about. Suddenly, that possibility seemed more folly than fabulous. What could a small town chef have in common with a man who had his sailboat delivered a thousand miles—in case he felt the urge to use it?

Some of what she was feeling must have shown in her eyes. Because he took her hand and lowered her until she was sitting on the bed.

He sat beside her and brushed a fingertip over her cheek. "It's just a boat, Meggy. An entertainment. I've been lucky enough to have been given opportunities in my life, but I've also worked hard to achieve what I have. The money is nice, it makes things convenient, but I'm still a man like any other. I'm still the same man I was last night."

Just a boat? His easy dismissal of such incomprehensible wealth showed the distance between their worlds for the uncrossable chasm it was. Inadequate and outclassed, how could a struggling chef from a middle class upbringing find balance with a creature of privilege? Pride battled pragmatism, leaving her adrift in confusion.

With nerves tightening her belly, her eyes scanned the room once more. She gestured around the cabin with her free hand, hoping she could make him understand. "I don't have any experience with this kind of lifestyle, Trevor." The reality of her words made her unbelievably sad. "You live in a different world than I do."

He raised the hand he held, turning it up to press a kiss to her palm. "I live in your carriage house, Meggy." He smiled that crooked smile of his, the one that sent her pulse bumping. His gray eyes were steady. "And today, I'm taking a beautiful fairy sailing. Later, I hope to share a romantic dinner with her, or perhaps another naked picnic, where I can charm her into spending even more time with me."

In spite of her misgivings, she couldn't help but smile. His wealth and the differences it represented in their lives was something she would have to deal with eventually, but not today. Today, she simply wanted to enjoy a lovely sail with a sexy man. "I'm afraid the picnic will have to wait. Today is Cara's birthday. We're having a birthday dinner at the Finnegans' at six." He looked so disappointed she had to laugh. "I was hoping I could talk you into coming along. Finn will be there, and

Erin's Ryan. I think you'll enjoy meeting them both."

"You've twisted my arm." He dropped a quick kiss on her lips. "It's a date. Now, let's get this show on the road. The tide waits for no one."

\*\*\*\*

"That came for you while you were gone." Shan jerked her chin toward a package sitting on the bar where she was doing inventory.

From across the dining room, Meggy could see the small box wrapped in pale blue paper with a silver ribbon. She changed direction in mid-stride. "For me?"

"That's what the delivery man said."

She wrenched off her sweatshirt as she approached the bar, tossing it across the back of a stool. Grinning, she picked up the box and examined it, turning it this way and that. She held it up to her ear and shook it.

"Oh, for crying out loud," Shan complained. "Open it already. I've been staring at that thing for the last three hours!"

She laughed and ripped at the ribbon and paper.

Shan leaned forward for a closer look.

When she flipped open the lid, startled laughter escaped her lips. She lifted the sterling silver bracelet from its bed and held it up for Shan to see. A single charm dangled. "It's a picnic basket!" Her smile was so wide, her cheeks hurt. And her heart did a delighted, slow somersault. Every cell in her body sighed.

"I can see that." Shan flicked the tiny silver basket with a fingertip. "It's adorable. Who's it from?"

"Trevor." Meggy sighed, her smile still wide as she held it up to the light.

"Why a picnic basket? What's it mean?"

"I've told you before, I don't kiss and tell." She

knew the heat of the blush that rose on her cheeks spoke volumes.

"Hmmm," Shan hummed in understanding, rushing to help when she struggled to clasp the bracelet around her wrist. "It's a smart man who knows how to remind a woman of a sexy memory without words. You're toast, Meggy."

She nodded and laughed at Shan's remark, holding out her arm to better admire Trevor's gift. If he kept doing things like this, she certainly would be. All day long, he'd been charming and funny, and he'd made her forget all about the differences in their backgrounds. By the time they'd returned to the marina, she'd been all but floating with pleasure. She was still floating.

With his reminder of last night sparkling on her wrist, she decided Trevor Bryce had some very sweet ideas. She couldn't wait to thank him.

"I guess I don't have to ask if you had fun today."

"No, you don't. It was wonderful, but..." The pleasure of the afternoon dimmed when she recalled the evidence of his wealthy background.

"But?"

"He's loaded, Shan. You should see his boat. It's a frigging yacht."

"Why does that require a 'but'?"

Meggy ran a fingertip over the delicate bracelet. "It doesn't, really. It's just that I realized you guys were right this morning. I don't know anything about him, and if he's as rich as that boat indicates, I don't have anything in common with him either."

Shan pointed a finger at the tiny charm. "Apparently, you both enjoy picnics."

She snorted, but had to smile. "You know what I

mean."

"Yeah, I do. But just because he comes from a different social set doesn't mean the two of you can't be right for one another. You say you aren't in love with him—"

"Yet..." She turned soulful eyes on her friend. "Yet."

"Yet. But you like him, right?"

She glanced at his gift on her wrist. "How can I help but like a man who would think of something like this?"

Shan raised a brow. "It's obvious he likes you too. Like you said, you don't know him all that well. Don't borrow trouble until you do. You may find you have more in common than you thought."

"I'm trying to tell myself that, but I have to admit, the money scares me. I keep thinking of Elizabeth Ashford and my birth mother. Money screws up people."

"You don't really know what the story is there. The Ashford money may have had nothing to do with Rachel Hadley's decision to give you up for adoption. It's not a good idea to draw any conclusions until you know all the facts."

"Aren't you the wise one?" She teased, scooping her sweatshirt from the stool.

The smile on Shan's face turned wry. "Yeah, that's me. The wise oracle of healthy relationships."

Meggy frowned at her friend. Though she'd finally begun to put it behind her after all this time, her ex-husband's infidelity and their consequent divorce was still a sore point with Shan.

Stepping back from the bar, she sobered. "There's a guy out there who will love you and your boys the way you deserve to be loved, Shan." She held out her arms, beaming. "Look at me. I was just minding my own business, painting a wall, and wham! Trevor walked into my life. Your job is to stay open to the possibilities."

"Yes, Ma," Shan drawled.

She snickered and turned on her heel to head upstairs. "Hey, maybe Trevor has a brother," she called over her shoulder laughing, but then her brows snapped together. Did he have any brothers? She'd have to ask him.

Chapter Twelve

Over the next week, Trevor came to learn that for a straightforward and strong woman, Meggy had a soft core of almost childlike appreciation for the life she'd built and the people with which she surrounded herself. She loved Palmerton and its residents and didn't hesitate to show it.

And Trevor wasn't excluded from her affectionate demonstrations; receiving more than a generous share of her tender attentions. He was humbled by her easy inclusion of him in her life, as though he belonged there. She didn't speak of love or any other feelings she might have for him, but she came into his arms whenever he reached for her. Her fairy smile continued to light up the room whenever their gazes met.

He'd taken to eating his dinner each night in the Palmer House lounge, conversing with the regulars and sampling the excellent cuisine while bellied up to the bar. With Meggy busy working her magic in the kitchen, he was content to sit and listen to the bits of gossip that came his way from the locals.

It was obvious from the pitying glances she sent his way from her place behind the bar that Shan noticed just how often his gaze strayed to the kitchen door. He couldn't bring himself to care. He loved watching his little fairy and was rewarded for his patience when she emerged from the kitchen each evening at eight.

Her sparkling blue eyes would seek him out and for a moment, her smile would be for him alone. Then, she'd turn her attention on her customers, charming her clientele like a magical sprite. When her tour of the dining area was completed, she'd stroll through the lounge, brushing her hand over his shoulder in silent greeting then stick out her tongue at Shan before returning to her kitchen.

The charm bracelet he'd had delivered the afternoon of their sail was a definite hit. Meggy loved the whimsy of it and had shown her appreciation by leading him to his bed that evening with a sultry smile. In the flickering firelight, she'd proceeded to shed herself of every stitch of clothing until she stood before him like a golden, glowing candle, wearing nothing but his gift. He grew hard thinking of the pleasurable hours they'd spent that night—and each one since.

The next evening, she'd stopped at the bar to kiss him lightly on the lips, ignoring Shan's throat clearing. With a whisper, she'd thanked him for the tiny, silver fairy that had joined the picnic basket at her wrist that afternoon. She'd grinned and mussed his hair, much to the patrons' growing amusement, the night the sparkling Celtic's mascot was added to the charm collection.

As if word of his daily gifts had spread, the number of locals appearing at the bar each night, just before eight, swelled until the patrons were standing three deep, waiting for Palmer House's chef to emerge from the kitchen wearing her latest charm. The nosy residents of Palmerton didn't even try to hide their interest in "the writer's" courtship of Meggy Calhoun.

Each night that week, she stopped by his stool to thank him for the newest trinket he had delivered daily.

While Shan rolled her eyes at the spectacle, Meggy would present her wrist to the growing crowd. With a fairy smile on her wide mouth, she displayed the miniature whisk, the sailboat, and the chef's hat.

Applause and laughter had those in the dining room craning their necks at the commotion the night the gleaming lady juggler joined the other charms. Meggy, in her chef's smock, skipped the tour of tables that night to head straight for him. Her laughing gaze never left his as she crossed the room. Climbing into his lap with a throaty laugh, she winked at the cheering crowd, and proceeded to plant a very unprofessional kiss on his grinning lips.

His wooing of Meggy Calhoun was proceeding according to plan, but she still hadn't told him she loved him. Tonight's charm was designed to rectify that. If he was to see Meggy wave her flag before the truth came to light, it would have to. Elizabeth's patience had run out.

****

The hour was late and Meggy was tired when they left Palmer House. She floated in pleasant lassitude as Trevor drove them to a surprise location. A grin curled her lips when he pulled into the marina parking lot. The idea of having Trevor all to herself for the next thirty-six hours sent shivers of excitement through her, dispelling her weariness. She'd been fantasizing about having him alone on his boat and in his big bed since the day he'd taken her for a sail.

Aboard Christos' Chariot, he led her directly below. She caught her breath when he opened the door to the cabin. Candlelight bathed the soft wood of the walls, and when her gaze moved to the bed, it was to find the coverlet turned down in invitation. Wine chilled in a bucket on the side table.

Her heart did a slow roll in her chest. Like a conquering marauder, he'd battered against her misgivings over the past week, showering her with thoughtfulness and his gently teasing attentions. Though she'd been able to deny her ever-insistent voice of reason up to now, she no longer could. She slid across the chasm with barely a whisper—and found love.

Her heart throbbing with her newly realized emotion, she turned to smile. "You've been busy."

He dropped their overnight bags at the foot of the bed and moved toward her. "I had help. I wanted everything set when we arrived so there would be no delay when I did this." His mouth swooped down on hers hungrily, and the heat she'd come to expect at his slightest touch burst into flame.

His mouth on hers was ravenous, as though he'd been starving for the taste of her. She knew the feeling. She'd been just as starved. Under his nimble fingers, the buttons of her top gave and the silky material of her blouse slithered from her shoulders to pool on the floor. Her slacks joined it with amazing speed. He stepped back to look down at her, and she saw him swallow. Without a word, he lowered her to the mattress and joined her, his body pressed to her side.

His fingers were urgent as he nipped and tugged at her bra and panties, frantically shedding her of the last barrier of clothing. It wasn't until he had her completely naked that he gentled his touch. Propped up on one elbow, he stroked her from neck to knees, his eyes darkening as he stoked the fire in her until she reached critical mass. She exploded like a roman candle on the fourth of July, his name on her lips as she shattered beneath his talented fingers.

He was leaning over her, watching her with a stormy gaze when she finally came back to herself. Her arms leaden, they lay limply above her head, refusing to move. She smiled up at him.

"Why aren't you naked? I've dreamed about having you naked in this bed."

His eyes flashed with an answering heat. "I'm sorry, Meggy." He leaned down to drop a kiss on her nose. "Ripping off your clothes before I'd even shut the door wasn't in my plans for tonight."

"It's good to know you can think outside the box." She grinned at his guilty smile. "I wasn't exactly complaining, Trevor. Though I might start if I don't see some of that sexy skin of yours really soon."

Rolling away from her, he stood.

She propped herself up against the pillows and sat back to enjoy the impromptu striptease he provided as he shed himself of his clothes like a man on a mission. "So." She swallowed at the sight of the heavy bulge beneath his navy briefs, and had to begin again. "So, if getting me naked wasn't in your plans for tonight, what was?"

He looked up from where he searched through the pocket of his jeans to give her a leering grin. "Oh, getting you naked was always part of the plan." He came toward her to sit at her hip on the side of the bed. "I just planned for that to wait until after I gave you this." He held out his hand.

She leaned forward to see what rested on his palm, then traced a fingertip over the fat, silver heart. As the previous ones had, his latest addition to her bracelet shot a rush of giddy warmth through her. "It's beautiful,

Trevor."

When she would have plucked it from his palm, he closed his fingers around the trinket. Her confused gaze flew up to meet his.

"Do you know what this is?"

She nodded. "It's a heart. I love it, Trevor."

"I'm glad to hear that." His hand remained fisted. "But it's not just a heart."

"It's not?"

His fingers unfurled. "Look at it, Meggy." He waited until she had. "It looks solid and it's built strong, but it can be broken."

She met his intense gaze and held her breath.

"I'm offering you my heart," he continued. "I'm hoping you'll take it with the knowledge that you have the power to crush it."

Though she wanted to laugh and jump into his arms, she didn't. She couldn't, not with her future happiness looming before her. Not when he was looking so serious. Besides, she needed to be sure she understood what he was saying. She took a deep breath. "I'm in love with you, Trevor," she said quietly, and pressed her fingers to the slow smile that spread on his lips to stop him from responding. "I never expected to find a man who would make me feel the way you do. I'll take your heart, but only if you'll take mine as well. I want your love, Trevor. I'll settle for nothing less."

The tiny heart sparkled in the lamplight as he held out his open hand. "Fairy girl, I love you more than I ever knew a man could love a woman."

With a grin, she plucked the tiny trinket from his palm and did what she'd wanted to do. She shrieked with laughter and jumped, naked, into his arms.

Chapter Thirteen

Meggy woke to the soft lapping of waves against the hull of Christos' Chariot. Eyes closed, she stretched like a sultry cat, basking in the warmth of Trevor's bed. Her eyes popped open upon recalling where she was. She sat up straight, only to find the bunk beside her empty.

Early morning light illuminated the charm bracelet that was all she wore. She stretched out her bare arm to admire it. The fat heart had joined his other gifts sometime during the night, when he'd insisted he wanted her in nothing but her charms. He'd grinned as he made the request, with its double entendre, and pleased them both by spending the next few hours sampling those charms.

Pure joy burst in her heart. She flopped back against the pillow, pulling the sheet and comforter up over her head to indulge in uncontrollable glee by wriggling and squealing beneath the covers like a little girl on Christmas morning. She was still grinning at her foolishness when she poked her head out to see if her little celebration had alerted Trevor that she was awake. The room was still empty.

Trevor Bryce loved her. She shook her head where it lay, smiling at the ceiling. He hadn't asked her to marry him, but he would. And when he did, she'd say yes. Yes! Yes! Yes! Man, she really was a goner.

The stray thought had her sitting up straight. "I need to call Cara!" Her voice was loud in the silence of the room.

Tangled in the covers, her gaze searched the room for the clutch purse she'd carried the night before. She spotted it on the chair in the corner. At the same moment, she swung her legs over the side of the bed to go collect it and her cell phone, the door opened.

"You're awake." Trevor crossed the room to the bed, handing her the coffee mug he carried. He covered her mouth with his in a sweet morning greeting.

"Good morning." She smiled when he stepped away to pick up her overnight bag.

Already dressed himself, he returned to the bed with the jeans and sweater she'd packed for this morning. He held them out.

Without thought, she took them. "Wouldn't you like to come back to bed for a little while?" She batted her eyelashes and exaggerated her best sultry look, then spoiled it by grinning.

Though his eyes darkened, he didn't smile. "More than you know. Unfortunately, we don't have time. I'll leave you to dress. Meet me on deck when you're ready." He turned without another word.

She scrambled to her knees. "Trevor?"

He turned back to her.

Although it had to be her imagination, she thought his smile looked forced.

"It'll be all right, Meggy. I'll see you on deck." The door to the cabin closed behind him with a quiet snick.

It'll be all right? What would be all right? What was wrong? She climbed from the bunk and began pulling on her clothes. After yanking a brush through her hair, she searched through her bag for her toothbrush and quickly brushed her teeth in the basin. Without another thought, she grabbed her clutch from the chair and headed up on deck.

Trevor stood at the rail. He turned when she stepped out into the chilly morning air. His hair ruffled in the breeze.

She took a moment to appreciate how handsome he looked in worn jeans and a faded Harvard sweatshirt. Harvard? Had he gone to Harvard?

She decided right then and there that she was sitting him down and asking him all those pertinent questions she'd neglected to ask because she'd been so busy floating in the clouds over the way he made her feel. But first she meant to find out what he'd meant by that "everything will be all right" comment.

The question vanished from her mind as she noted their surroundings. Expecting an array of masts, and the bustling activity of Charlestown marina, she was bewildered at the sight of a serenely quiet stretch of sandy beach off to the right and the rocky cliff beyond. To the left, a lush lawn, beginning to yellow with the season sloped inland, and her gaze landed on the sprawling edifice perched at the top of the rise. A resort?

Disoriented, she accepted the hand Trevor held out to her and followed when he stepped from the boat to the dock. "Where are we? How did we get here?"

"We set sail after you fell asleep last night." His hand on her elbow, he led her down the dock to the crushed shell path leading up to the resort. "There's someone I need you to meet."

"Who?" Though wary, she matched his step along the path.

"My grandmother."

She skidded to a halt and tugged her arm free of his grasp. "Your grandmother? Right now? Trevor, I can't meet your grandmother. I look horrible!" She hadn't even taken the time to wash her face, and she still wore the dregs of last night's makeup. Her gaze swung beyond him to the house she'd assumed was a resort, and she groaned.

He grabbed her hand and began tugging her up the hill. "You look beautiful." His gaze ran over her face. "Gorgeous. Besides, Grandmother knows we're here. She's waiting for us. She'll come charging down here herself if we don't make an appearance in the parlor in two minutes."

"Just let me..."

"It'll be fine, Meggy," he repeated, tugging her toward a set of gleaming French doors at the top of the shelled pathway.

He was springing her on his grandmother without any warning, and he thought everything would be fine? Oh, yeah, there were some things Trevor Bryce was going to learn about *her* as well. She'd be all too happy to enlighten him...if she didn't belt him first.

The doors opened onto a long, wide hallway. Trevor didn't hesitate. He continued to pull her toward some unknown point.

She took no notice of their surroundings, too busy rubbing stiff fingers at the skin under her eyes. Had her mascara smudged while she'd slept? After his odd comment, she hadn't even glanced in a mirror, so she had no idea.

Forget belting him, she was going to *kill* him.

All too soon he was stepping to the side, and using

his hand on the small of her back, he gave her a gentle nudge that sent her through a doorway into a truly impressive room.

Decorated in classic, New England farmhouse, the walls were glossy white, the floor a stunning, wide plank. Vintage, leaden-glass windows let in the morning light in rippling beams, illuminating the inviting seating area with its sleek, feminine furniture.

Beside a working fireplace that took up a good portion of the far wall, a small, expensively dressed woman with a shock of styled, white hair sat in an upholstered chair. She rose when Meggy stepped into the room.

Grandmother Bryce, she mused. The woman was staring at her so intently, Meggy was afraid she had more to worry about than just a little smudged makeup. As stealthily as she could manage, she slid her fingers to the zipper of her jeans, and nearly laughed in relief to find it closed properly.

"Welcome home, Mr. Christos," a feminine voice spoke from somewhere at Meggy's back. She started, not having noticed there was anyone else in the room. Her head jerked in the direction of the voice to find a young maid nodding to Trevor before slipping out of the room. She shut the door behind her.

A glance around the room revealed only one Mr., and that was Trevor. Mr. Christos? Why would the woman call Trevor by the wrong name?

Christos? Christos' Chariot? Uneasiness tickled at her spine. When she'd asked him about the name of his boat, he'd explained it was a family name. He hadn't said it was *his* name. Her gaze tangled with his. "Mr. *Christos*?"

He didn't have a chance to answer.

The door opened to admit yet another woman, and Meggy's eyes widened in horrified disbelief. Elizabeth Ashford's housekeeper stared back, looking as confused as Meggy felt. Forget uneasiness, she was going to throw up! She spun on her heel. Her gaze collided with the crystal blue gaze of the older woman whom she realized with sickening dread must be none other than her biological great-grandmother.

"Why don't we all sit down?"

Meggy slapped at the hand Trevor held out. She stumbled several feet away. *Oh, God.*

"Megan." Elizabeth Ashford's quiet voice drew her attention. "My grandson is right. We should all—"

"Grandson?" Meggy yelped. Her gaze darted from Trevor to Elizabeth and back again. An odd buzzing echoed in her ears and the light in the room seemed to fade even as she put her hand to her head to counteract the tipping sensation.

Right there in Elizabeth Ashford's exquisite parlor, Meggy Calhoun did something she'd never done in her life. She fainted.

Chapter Fourteen

Meggy opened her eyes and stared at a high, intricately carved ceiling. Trevor's worried face, swimming into view, made her slam her eyelids shut on a groan. She hadn't been dreaming after all. She was living a nightmare.

"She's coming around."

Meggy's eyes popped open. Twisting her head back and around, she searched for the owner of the voice. Inches above hers, she found the smiling face of the bulky bodyguard she'd met several weeks ago. "If it isn't the mountainous menace."

The bodyguard chuckled. He laid a cool cloth across her brow. "Nice to see you again too."

"Give her some room, Brody," Trevor barked.

The demand reminded her he was sitting on the couch, his hip pressed against hers. Oh, God. He'd lied about his name, and considering just *whose* couch they were on, she doubted she'd be pleased with his explanation of why.

He was Elizabeth Ashford's grandson. What did that make her, his niece?

Her head was too mushy to think. All she knew for certain was that Trevor Bryce had suddenly become Trevor Christos, and she was going to throw up on Elizabeth Ashford's highly polished, wooden floor. While she was at it, she'd aim for *Uncle* Trevor's shoes.

She shoved at him, swinging her legs to the floor and sitting up. The cool cloth plopped to her lap. A hand to her chest, shoving her back down, kept her from standing.

Trevor pointed a finger in her face. "Just sit there and be quiet."

"*You* be quiet." She slapped away his hand. "I don't have to listen to you. You're not the boss of me."

"I said, sit there and be quiet." Trevor propped his hands onto his hips. "I'm not having you faint on me again."

"Bite me, Mr. *Christos*." She spoke through gritted teeth.

Brody chuckled behind her, but Trevor simply raised a sardonic brow.

"Where's my purse?" she demanded on a sudden gust of breath.

"It's right beside you on the couch." The strong voice of Elizabeth Ashford came from the chair beside her.

Meggy had no idea what to say to the woman, so she ignored her, scrambling to pull her cell phone from the clutch bag.

"Who are you calling?"

Ignoring Trevor wasn't as easy, not when she wanted to scratch out his eyes.

"Nine-one-one." She released the lock on the phone. "I don't know what's going on here, but kidnapping and holding people against their will is a crime." She glanced around the room. "Even for people like you."

"Give me that." Trevor snatched the phone from her hand.

"Hey!"

"No one is holding you against your will, Megan." Elizabeth's voice was calmness itself.

Meggy didn't even glance her way, pointing at Trevor. "Tell that to him!" She seared him with a narrowed glare. "On second thought, you probably own the local police. I'll call the FBI."

Elizabeth sighed. "You haven't handled the situation very well, darling. The girl is terrified."

"She's not terrified, Grandmother, she's pissed. She's a pit bull." He snorted. "She'll get over it."

Meggy jerked back against the couch, absorbing the unexpected lash of pain his words brought. On Trevor's lips, there wasn't anything remotely amusing about her nickname.

"Jesus." Trevor squeezed the bridge of his nose. "Everyone just calm down for a minute."

"That's good advice, Trev."

Trevor turned an icy glare on Brody. He simply shrugged, his smile casual. Trevor held out her phone. "My Grandmother has some questions for you."

"I'll just bet she does." She snatched the phone from his fingers with a sneer. "I have a few of my own."

"Then stick around and get the answers."

"Why am I here?" She had to know. She needed the facts, all of them.

Instead of answering, he asked his own question. "Why were you here a month ago?"

Her heart thudded frantically while plunging to her stomach. He'd known she'd come here to the farm all those weeks ago? If he'd known she'd been here, then his showing up in Palmerton hadn't been coincidence. He'd known who she was, and he'd come looking for her. And, oh, God, she had taken one look at him and had fallen like a stone. Only, none of it had been real.

She'd been afraid she wouldn't like what she found inside these gilded walls, and she'd been right. Going to her parents with her questions had been a colossal mistake, and she was going to burn Rachel Hadley's letter the moment she got home. In the meantime, she had no choice but to brazen it out, even though all she wanted to do was run. "I came looking for a job," she spat.

"Cut the crap, Meggy. No one in this room believes that. What were you looking for that day?"

"I was looking for something that doesn't exist," she said tightly. At his scowl, she turned to look directly at Elizabeth Ashford for the first time since she'd awakened from her faint. "I'm adopted. I received a letter from my birth mother, a Rachel Hadley." She continued speaking over Elizabeth's indrawn breath. "She said I had a great-grandmother living on Martha's Vineyard. I was curious." She shook her head helplessly and fought against the unexpected urge to weep. "I just came to see."

Out of the corner of her eye, she saw Trevor moving toward her and jumped to her feet. She held out a stiff arm to prevent him from coming any closer. "So, now I've seen. I don't want anything. Not from any of you." Meggy pivoted for the door.

Elizabeth rose to her feet. "Stay, Megan. You're upset."

Her throat was tight, but her eyes were dry when she paused and turned back. "I'm sorry for the pretense, Mrs. Ashford. I just wanted to see where my birth mother came from." She whirled to make good her escape.

Trevor had moved to block her way. "I'll take you home. We need to talk."

She fried him with a lethal glare. "I don't ever want to see *you* again," she said softly, her words evenly spaced.

Cold and angry, his gaze dropped to her wrist and the fat heart dangling there. He met her gaze, and his brows rose in wordless accusation.

Her fingers clamped around the bracelet, and she cringed at the reminder of what a fool he'd made of her, of all of them. Without looking away, she released the clasp on the charm bracelet and held it out to him. He refused to take it from her, so she leaned around him to drop it to the coffee table. It made a tinkling clatter in the silence of the room.

His eyes were bright with fury when she straightened. "You're not going anywhere." He lowered his voice so that only she could hear. "This situation isn't comfortable, or easy, for any of us." His gaze flicked briefly to Elizabeth. He lowered his voice even more. "You'd realize that if you'd quit acting like a rude little brat."

"Rude..." she sputtered, "Brat?"

He didn't pause in his ultimatum. "Now park your sweet little ass on that couch." He flung an arm in the direction of the couch where she'd been sitting. "We're going to sit down and discuss this like reasonable adults."

She gave him no warning. Her balled fist plowed into his unprotected stomach. Though she was sure she'd hurt her hand worse than she'd hurt him, she was satisfied with his surprised grunt. She took advantage of his startled shock to find her way out the front door and didn't look back.

****

"That went well."

"Shut up, Brody." Trevor glared at the man he'd considered a friend since childhood.

Brody just raised a brow and grinned.

"Behave yourselves. Both of you." Elizabeth's tone booked no room for argument as she lowered herself to her chair.

Despite the disastrous results of the meeting, Elizabeth wore a satisfied smile. He knew she thrilled to have the question of Meggy's identity all but answered. They may never find Rachel, but they'd found her daughter, or more to the fact, her daughter had found them.

He moved to the window in time to see Meggy hurrying at a near run down the long driveway toward the front gate. She had a letter from Rachel. It would have to be verified, of course, but the matter was settled in his mind. The woman he'd fallen in love with was Elizabeth's great-granddaughter.

When Meggy fainted, he'd never felt so scared in his life. His heart had literally stopped. Damn, he hated situations where he wasn't in control. Yet, that's what his fairy girl had done to him, taken his composure and love to leave him desolate and empty.

Following her progress down the drive, he watched her stomp her way up to the gate, her cell phone pressed to one ear. She slapped a hand to the gate release and squeezed through before it had swung open completely.

It crossed his mind that Rachel had taken the same path so many years ago. She'd stepped through that gate, and they'd never seen her again. His tender stomach muscles contracted in unreasonable panic. He loved her too much to lose her, but how was he to smooth her ruffled feathers and get her to forgive him? "Brody," he said without turning from the window. "Take the car. Get her home."

"What if she refuses? That is one *pissed-off* woman."

Trevor glanced over his shoulder at Brody and the straining muscles evident beneath his lightweight suit. "Convince her." He turned back to the window in time to see her disappear around the wall. "I'm holding you responsible for her safety."

Brody left without another word.

He turned to find Elizabeth staring blindly into space, a smile on her lips. "She's Rachel's daughter, Trevor," she whispered.

He moved to squat in front of her, taking her chilled hands in his. "Yes, she is."

Her eyes filled with tears as they focused on his face. "She wants nothing to do with us. That's unacceptable. What do you suggest we do to change that?"

He gazed at the thin hands in his and sighed. He'd bungled things with his snarling and ultimatums. But he'd never reacted well to confusion, and the terrified look on her face when she realized just where she was had confused the hell out of him. Anger he could have handled. Her fear he couldn't understand.

"I'm going back to Palmerton. I need to see that letter. So do you. After that?" He shrugged.

"What happened?" Elizabeth raised a wrinkled hand slightly before letting it fall back into her lap. "Why was she so angry? And she looked scared."

Trevor stood and pushed a hand through his hair in agitation. "She was terrified. I have no idea what that was about. But I'd say she was as much hurt as she was angry." His smile was a twisted contortion of guilt. "I, uh, got her to admit she's in love with me just last night."

"Oh, Trevor."

"I had a plan," he said in self-defense. "It looks like it may have backfired."

"I should say so." She watched him with keen eyes. "Are you in love with her?"

"Yes." He took a seat across from her. "And up until about fifteen minutes ago, she was in love with me. Well," he corrected, "technically, she was in love with Trevor Bryce."

"No wonder she's angry. No woman enjoys learning she's been lied to by the man she loves." She shook her head. "What a mess."

"I've had the same thought myself." He went on to tell her all he'd learned in his three weeks in Palmerton. "She's led a good life, Grandmother. She's surrounded by friends and family who love and think the world of her." He frowned. "I'll be lucky if they don't run me out of town on a rail."

"It sounds as if she's worth the trouble." She grinned, and he nodded. "Rachel's daughter," she repeated with a happy sigh.

Chapter Fifteen

With bare hands, Meggy gripped at the metal rail. Twenty feet below, water churned by as the crowded ferry chewed through the choppy waves toward the mainland. In just her sweater and jeans, she was freezing in the autumn wind. Her thoughts, however, were steaming hot.

Her great-grandmother's bodyguard—a term she would never have expected to use in connection with herself—had all but forced her into a silver Bentley less than a quarter mile from Ashford Farm. The mountainous menace had intimidated her after all, threatening bodily transport into the passenger seat, if she didn't get herself there immediately. She'd been forced to call Cara back to let her know she had a ride home and would see her at Palmer House in a few hours.

She sensed the bodyguard's presence as he came up behind her.

He dropped an oversized trench coat over her shoulders, then leaned his elbows on the rail beside her.

"Thank you," she said grudgingly, shoving her arms through the sleeves before tucking her hands in the pockets.

He nodded. "You must have questions. Why not stick around and get the answers?"

Breath exploded through her nose on a disdainful snort. "Like I'd believe anything that lying son of a bitch came up with. I don't want anything from you people. Including answers."

His chuckle was deep and genuine. "You're Mrs. A's blood all right. She's just as stubborn."

She accepted the challenge in his words. "It's not your Mrs. A. who makes me want to take a flame thrower to that mansion you live in. She's nothing to me but a name in a letter. It's that lying bastard grandson of hers."

Brody turned to lean a hip against the rail.

The grin on his face made her roll her eyes in annoyance. Then her own words registered, and she felt the return of panic, remembering she'd not only fallen in love with a liar, but a relative. "I've changed my mind." Pivoting, she met his gaze directly. "I do have one question. Trevor is her grandson, and if that letter is true, I'm her great-granddaughter. So what does that make me, his niece?" She paled as a new thought occurred. "Oh God, don't tell me he's my father!" Her eyes slid shut and her shoulders slumped almost immediately. "No, there's no way he could be my father. He's too young." She glanced back at Brody, who was doing his best not to laugh. "So, *is* he my uncle?"

Brody lost the fight. He laughed, deep and full. "You find a great-grandmother worth almost a billion dollars and all you want to know is how you're related to Trevor?"

The wry look in his eyes said he knew exactly what had been going on between her and his employer for the past few weeks. She mentally added blabbermouth to her list of charges against the lying bastard—who may or may not be her uncle.

"You know, Meggy—you don't mind if I call you

Meggy, do you?" Brody continued before she could demand he answer her question. "You're going to have to do a better job of hiding your feelings if you're going to exact any kind of revenge before you forgive him."

She ignored his knowing grin. "He doesn't deserve my forgiveness. And I'll have to settle for that one punch as revenge since I don't plan to ever see the bastard again. Unless you tell me he came to Palmerton and made me...unless he played out his little charade knowing he really *is* my uncle. Then I'd have to kill him. So, *is* he?"

Brody snorted a laugh. "You really are a pit bull. Poor Trevor."

"Just answer the frigging question." She gritted her teeth at his continued chuckling.

"You can relax, Meggy. Trevor is Rachel's step-brother. His father married Rachel's mother. You're no relation that I know of."

She puffed out a relieved breath. Well, that was something. At least, she wasn't guilty of incest. That left the bastard off on that charge. It didn't excuse him for all the others though.

"And I wouldn't count on having seen the last of him, if I were you." His words yanked her from her musings. He held up a hand when she would have argued his point. "Think about it, Meggy. We're not just talking about a misunderstanding between two consenting adults here. They've been searching for word of Mrs. A's granddaughter for a quarter century. If that letter you mentioned is legit, you're more than just word, you're DNA. Do you really think they'll just forget about that?"

She had no argument, so she made none.

"Even if Trevor didn't have a personal interest in you." His raised brow challenged her to deny his point. She didn't bother. "There are close to three quarters of a billion reasons for them to want to verify your identity."

She blanched. "I don't want anything to do with their money. Tell them I'll sign whatever they want. I'll promise not to ever ask them for a thing."

His brows rose, but he shook his head. "Mrs. A. isn't going to let the matter drop. She'll be all over you—and that letter—before the week is out."

"I'm burning it the minute I get home."

That gave him pause, and the perpetual grin slipped from his face. "Don't do that, Meggy. Mrs. A. is a tough old bird. She's had to be. But she's a human being, and deep down she has a soft heart." His sentiment echoed Trevor's description of his grandmother the night of their first date. "She's lost or buried everyone she's ever cared about with very few exceptions. Trevor being the most notable. That letter is a link to her granddaughter. Are you really willing to take that away?"

Her silence was answer enough.

He nodded. "Besides…" The smile returned. "Trevor would be pissed if you destroyed it."

"You think?" She offered her sweetest smile. "You almost had me convinced not to burn it. Now, I'm going to have to give it some more thought."

Brody threw back his head and laughed. "You're a bloodthirsty little thing, aren't you?"

She smiled, a simple baring of her teeth.

"Poor Trevor."

For several moments, she was silent. "What exactly did he hope to achieve by showing up in Palmerton and pretending to be someone he isn't?"

"That's two." Brody held up two cigar-shaped fingers.

"Two?"

"Questions. I thought you didn't have any."

She decided it wouldn't take much to learn to hate this man. "You're right." She sniffed and turned to study a brightly painted lighthouse on a cliff in the distance. "Forget I asked."

His long sigh was full of regret and apology in one. "Look, Meggy. I work for Trevor, but he's also a friend. He has a reason for everything he does. If you want to know what those reasons are, you have to ask him."

She didn't say another word, not even "thank you" when he delivered her to Palmer House two hours later.

****

"I'll kill him! I want directions to that farm, Meggy." Cara paced the hardwood floor in Shan's kitchen. "Never mind. Martha's Vineyard isn't that big, I'll find it myself. You can drive me, Erin. I'm liable to run him down the moment I see him."

Erin smiled wryly at her sister. "We can't have that. I'm not sure how Finn would feel about conjugal visits with you doing time."

"You're not helping, ladies." Shan popped the cork from a bottle of wine.

"Says who?" Three identical green gazes turned on Meggy. She shrugged. "Picturing Trevor Bryce—make that Trevor Christos—with his body broken and bloody sure makes *me* feel better."

The O'Shea sisters had reacted to this morning's revelations with varying degrees of disbelief and outrage. Though she'd tried, she couldn't seem to settle on one emotion. She felt like she was suffering from a

110

raging case of PMS. Since she'd spotted the Ashford housekeeper and realized the last few weeks had been nothing but an elaborate ruse, she'd been catapulted back and forth between red hot fury and the uncontrollable urge to weep, with a healthy dose of fear thrown in for good measure. She was doing her best to stay focused on the fury.

"I can't believe it." Shan pulled glasses from a cabinet, pouring wine into the crystal. "He sat in the bar every night and talked to me. He asked me all kinds of questions about you. About when we were growing up. I thought he was infatuated. I even thought it was kind of sweet." She sipped and waved her glass toward Meggy. "I can't believe the jerk was pumping me for information all along."

"I can't believe any of it. I know he lied about who he was, Meggy." Erin's eyes filled with helpless apology. "But a man doesn't look at a woman the way Trevor looks at you if he doesn't have feelings. I can't believe it was all just pretense."

"Well, believe it," Meggy said sharply. She reached for the wine bottle on the table and topped off Shan's glass, then refilled Erin's. Cara had said she was too upset to drink. She emptied the remainder of the bottle into her own glass. "According to Brody, Trevor is Elizabeth Ashford's golden boy. He'd do anything for her. When I showed up at the farm, she sent him to find out everything he could about me."

"*She* sent him?" Cara paused in her pacing.

Meggy shrugged. "She sent him...he came himself. What difference does it make? They recognized me and decided on a preemptive strike before I tried to cash in on their empire."

She'd learned that much when to her surprise, Finn had recognized the Ashford bodyguard the moment they'd pulled into the driveway. It always surprised her how small the world really was. The world of pro football was even smaller. As an ex-strong-safety for the New England Patriots, Brody hadn't exactly been a friend, but he'd rubbed shoulder pads with Finn, back when they'd both played in the NFL.

To her disgust, they'd shared a gridiron reunion, right there in her driveway. She'd flung the trench coat at the annoying bodyguard and stomped off in fury. Though Brody hadn't answered *all* of Finn's questions, he'd been happy to share what he could.

According to Brody, Meggy was the spitting image of her grandmother, Elizabeth Ashford's daughter, Anne. When she'd shown up at the farm several weeks ago, Elizabeth caught a glimpse of her. She'd given Trevor three weeks to find out what he could about her, and today had been the deadline.

"But why not just introduce himself and explain the situation?" Confusion wrinkled Shan's brow. "Why the subterfuge?"

"That's the billion dollar question," Meggy said bitterly. "Or *close* to a billion, if Brody can be believed."

"I vote we all go down to the carriage house and take a machete to his Armanis." At the three blank stares turned her way, Cara crossed her arms over her chest and shifted her shoulders. "But that's just me."

Meggy loved Cara's deep loyalty. "As tempting as that sounds, I think we'd better just pack up his stuff and have it delivered to the farm." She glanced around at her three closest friends, at her two partners. "Losing the rent on the carriage house is going to cut into our capital. I'll wave my paycheck until Jill can find us a new tenant."

"I don't think so," Cara growled. Shan shook her head.

"He only took the carriage house to get at me." Her trashed heart's shards were so sharp she could hardly breathe.

"And he signed a six-month lease," Cara reminded her. "It'll be a pleasure to sue him if he tries to break it."

She understood Cara's hostile anticipation of a little payback, but admitted, "I'd just assume we let the bastard break it." She paused. "But that's just me."

No one laughed at her attempt at humor.

Ever the voice of reason, Shan leaned on her elbows to say, "The lease aside, you said Brody believed they wouldn't let the identity issue drop. Trevor will be back, Meggy. And he won't be constrained by his guise as a charming writer this time. You'll be dealing with the billionaire's grandson. You need an attorney."

"I'll call mine." Cara took the last open chair at the table. "He's been known to eat small corporations for breakfast. I'm sure he'll be thrilled at the chance to take a big bite out of the Ashford pie."

"And I'll be permanently trapped in the Ashford crosshairs." Meggy shook her head. "No thanks. Call your lawyer, Cara. Shan's right, I'm going to need one, but only to draw up whatever papers are necessary to wave any and all connection to that family. Brody said they'll want Rachel Hadley's letter. They can have it, if they promise to leave me alone."

Chapter Sixteen

"You may want to get down here," Shan said the moment Meggy picked up the call on her cell phone.

"Why?"

"Look out the window."

Meggy scrambled to the tiny dormer window beside her bed. Early morning sunlight stabbed at her eyes, and she groaned at the sight of a black Mercedes and a silver Bentley parked at the end of the path leading to the carriage house. As she watched, Trevor stepped out of the Mercedes. He waved off Brody to help Elizabeth Ashford alight from the Bentley himself. With a hand on her elbow, he led her toward the main house. "Tell them I'm not here."

"I could do that, but even if Trevor believed me, which he won't, they'll be back, Meggy. And they're on *your* turf now. I'm here, and Cara and Erin can be here in two minutes. Wouldn't you rather face them and get it over with?"

She rolled her neck and shoulders and winced at the hot stab of pain flaring through her tensed muscles. The last twenty-four hours had only intensified the righteous anger that had kept her company throughout the long, sleepless night. Exhausted, her eyes scraped against her lids like high-grade sandpaper with every blink, but not from crying. A man willing to go to such extremes for his own selfish purposes wasn't worth a single tear, and she counted it a small victory that so far, she'd managed to defeat the tidal wave of grief threatening to drown her.

Embarrassment and fury gushed through her like a geyser as she watched Trevor and Elizabeth disappear beneath the portico's eve. Shan was right. The sooner she got the inevitable confrontation over with, the sooner she could put the entire sordid episode behind her and get on with her life. Why that thought would cause her airway to constrict, she refused to consider.

She attempted to jump-start her lungs with a breathy growl. "I hate it when you play the logic card."

Shan's laughter came through the phone. "They're at the door. What do you want me to do? Shall I hide behind the bar like a five-year-old, or do you want me to call my sisters?"

"Neither." She headed for the stairs. "I'm on my way down. And don't call your sisters. Cara is so mad she's libel to show up with that machete."

She pushed open the door from the kitchen, entering the dining room just as Elizabeth Ashford sank into an upholstered sofa in the lounge, guided gently by Trevor's hand on her elbow. Seeing him caused a spike of pain to slip past her anger. She swallowed and forced herself to cross the room.

Three gazes turned at the sound of her heels on the hardwood floor.

Shan shot her a sympathetic smile from the bar.

Elizabeth sat forward on the sofa, clutching a leather binder in her lap.

Trevor stood beside the sofa, his pale gaze passing over her from head to toe in a slow inspection.

The familiar once-over left her seething. He looked

confident and comfortable, standing with his hands tucked into the pockets of his black dress slacks. Only the stormy gray of his eyes indicated he considered this meeting more than just a casual gathering.

The sight of the overnight bag she'd left on board his boat, sitting at his feet, made her stomach cramp.

"I figured you'd refuse to see us—"

"And I would have, but someone convinced me this meeting was inevitable." She gave Shan a tight smile. "I decided to get it over and done with."

Trevor didn't respond. He looked to Shan where she stood with a hip leaning on a barstool. "Do we have you to thank for not having the door slammed in our faces?"

Shan shrugged, her gaze narrowed. "I didn't do it for you."

"I didn't think you had. I'm grateful just the same." He turned and held out a hand. "Will you sit?"

She had to move closer to him to enter the seating area and when she did, his voice dropped to a low rumble that only she could hear. "I'm sorry, fairy girl. So sorry."

She stiffened and turned from the entreaty in his eyes. Holding up the envelope containing Rachel's letter, she met the excitement in Elizabeth's. "I assume you're here for this. You can have it, *if* you promise never to do anything to harm me or my business. That includes my family and friends."

"Jesus, Meggy."

She continued to ignore him as if he weren't there. "My lawyer is drawing up documents denying any rights I might have to the Ashford millions. You can have your attorneys go over them to make sure I haven't slipped in any sneaky loopholes." She swept Trevor with a disdainful look. "When that's done, Rachel's letter will be delivered to you with your copies of the signed documents. I never want to see it again."

"Of all the stubborn..."

"Trevor," Elizabeth interrupted sharply without looking his way. "Why is it you assume we would do something to harm you, Megan?"

Her gaze flicked to Trevor. He didn't look calm or confident now. He looked frustrated and furious. She met Elizabeth's waiting gaze with a fierce one of her own. "Oh, I don't know." Sarcasm dripped from her every word. "Maybe because your first instinct on seeing me was to believe I was there to screw you somehow?"

"My first instinct," Elizabeth corrected, "was that you were my great-granddaughter." She opened the leather binder and pulled out a glossy photo. Her hand shook as she extended it. "Go ahead. Look at it."

Shan pushed away from the bar, stepping around the couch to look over Meggy's shoulder when she took the photo. "Wow."

She refrained from verbally echoing the sentiment, but she wholeheartedly agreed. The woman smiling back from the aged photograph could have been her twin. If she didn't know better, she would swear the photo was one of herself, taken without her knowledge.

"Yes, wow." Elizabeth nodded. "My daughter, Anne," she explained. "Your grandmother. You gave me quite a shock that day at the farm, and you'd disappeared before I regained my ability to speak."

She stared at the photo and understood the woman's shock. Her own face smiled back. But that didn't explain their deception of the last few weeks. "But you did regain the ability eventually," she glanced up to accuse, "enough to sic your wolfhound on me." Out of the corner of her eye, she saw Trevor bristle at the description. "You knew how to find me. A simple phone call would have confirmed I wanted nothing. Instead, you chose to spy on me in an effort to gain the upper hand on the evil golddigger."

"Grandmother isn't to blame here, Meggy," Trevor insisted.

She jerked her head around to fry him with her gaze. "Oh, I know exactly where to place the blame, *Uncle* Trevor."

He sighed. "I know you're angry, Meggy. You have every right to be, and I'll apologize again for the way things were handled. That was my doing. When you showed up at the farm the way you did, I assumed you were a fake." He lifted a hand to interrupt her when she hissed. "I was wrong. Everyone here now believes you really are Rachel's daughter and, as so, there are things we need to discuss. If you'll put aside your anger at me for a little while, we can do that."

She didn't see that there was anything to discuss, but she could see that they thought so. Fine. She'd decided to get this over with, and she would. Putting aside her anger was something else entirely. "I have no problem talking to you, Mrs. Ashford." She glared at Trevor. "You, on the other hand, I want no part of. In fact, now would be a perfect time for you to pack up your stuff and vacate the carriage house."

"Why would I do that?"

His calmness angered her all the more, if that were possible. "Because you won't be living there after today," she answered just as calmly.

He crossed his arms over his chest. "The lease agreement says I'll be living there for the next five months."

"I'm breaking your lease."

"I'll fight you on that, Meggy."

Her tentative control on her temper snapped. "Fine. Hire an attorney. Sue me. It'll be worth the cost to get rid of you."

"I don't have to hire an attorney. I'm licensed to practice law in Massachusetts."

That stopped her tirade, but only for a second. "An attorney?" She snorted in contempt. "That figures." She'd pegged him correctly that first day in the carriage house. Too bad she hadn't heeded her inner voice.

Elizabeth took advantage of the lull in their verbal skirmish. "Trevor, darling, we aren't accomplishing anything with the two of you snapping at each other. I'm sure you can find something to keep yourself occupied while Megan and I talk."

Though Meggy could see he wanted to argue against the dismissal, he nodded, and bent to press a kiss to Elizabeth's raised cheek. "I'll be in the carriage house." He aimed a hard glare at Meggy.

She averted her gaze, taking a seat across from Elizabeth and refusing to let her gaze follow him as he stalked out the front door.

"I'll make some coffee. You'll be okay?" Shan cast a worried gaze her way.

"I'll be fine, thanks."

Shan disappeared into the kitchen.

Squaring her shoulder, she met Elizabeth's gaze. "I'm listening. What do we have to discuss?"

Elizabeth shook her head and sighed. "You take

after Anne in more than just your looks. My daughter could have given mules stubborn lessons."

"According to Brody, she got that trait from you," she replied without hesitation and blinked when Elizabeth laughed.

"Yes, I suppose that's true." Elizabeth sat back and folded her wrinkled hands in her lap. "So, why do you hate me?"

"I don't hate you. I don't even know you."

"Distrust then."

"Can you blame me?"

"No, I can't." The older woman shook her head. "We misled you for our own purposes. The same way you misled Helen Smithers when you applied for the job at Ashford Farm."

She fought the urge to squirm under her intent regard. The truth of Elizabeth's words had guilt bumping against the wall of distrust Meggy had built, and she jutted her chin in defense. "I told you, I just wanted to see."

"I'll accept that excuse, if you'll accept that in our own way, we just wanted to see as well."

"Your way of seeing stinks," Meggy snapped. "I didn't intrude in your life, while you sent Trevor to...to pass himself off as a harmless stranger while he ingratiated himself with people I care about."

"And with you?"

The gleam in Elizabeth's eyes dared her to contradict her. The idea of just how far he had ingratiated himself with her was too humiliating to consider. She fell back on silence as her only safe response.

"I'll admit he could have handled the situation

better," Elizabeth said after a long moment.

"He could have simply asked." Her heart shredded a little more.

"Yes." Elizabeth nodded. "And considering what we all now know to be the truth, he should have done just that.

Meggy opened her mouth to agree.

Elizabeth held up her hand. "However, I understand why he didn't. You're not the first potential great-granddaughter to show up at the farm. Five years ago, a young woman arrived at the farm just as you did, only she wasn't there looking for a position. She claimed to be Rachel's child, and though I tried to remain impartial, at least until we'd established the legitimacy of her claim, she had the look of Rachel."

Her eyes took on a bitter glaze. "I wanted so badly to believe we'd found a part of Rachel, a part of Anne, that I didn't protect myself as I should. I was quite distraught when she disappeared rather than have the DNA testing to prove her claim conclusively." She glanced away for a few seconds and then sighed. "It took me months to recover. My despondency frightened Trevor. When you showed up at the farm, he saw it all happening again and did what he felt was necessary to protect me."

*And shredded me in the process.* The spiral of hurt that knowledge produced gathered steam until it was a physical ache in her chest. She forced herself to take several deep breaths in an effort to ease the pressure.

"Now, since we all believe your claim will be proven to be legitimate, tell me why you're afraid of me."

She had to take another of those deep breaths before

she could speak. "I thought I'd made it clear that I won't be making any claims. And I'm not afraid of you."

"You're terrified." Elizabeth's eyes narrowed. "You're Rachel's daughter. I don't understand why our accepting that fact frightens you."

"I'm not frightened," Meggy insisted and tried to believe it. "I'm pragmatic. I'm a small town chef from a middle-class upbringing. I don't understand the kind of existence that requires people to lie and deceive in an attempt to protect themselves. I never will. It would be best for all concerned if you'd just accept the papers I'm having drawn up and my word that I won't make any claim, and leave it at that."

Shan, bumping her way through the swinging door from the kitchen, drew their attention. They were silent as she placed the tray holding the coffee service on the table between them.

"Ah, reinforcements have arrived." Elizabeth pointedly nodded her head toward the three settings on the tray.

She lifted her chin and scowled at the humor dancing in Elizabeth's eyes.

"Shall I go?" Shan looked questioningly at her.

Elizabeth didn't give her the opportunity to answer. "Don't go on my account, my dear." She smiled at Shan. "I understand you are one of my great-granddaughter's partners."

"And friend." Shan took a seat beside her.

She swallowed at hearing herself called great-granddaughter by Elizabeth. Despite everything, the recognition of the relation being spoken so casually sent a shiver of something unexpected, and not completely unpleasant, tingling over her skin.

"Now, where were we?" Elizabeth accepted a cup and saucer from Shan. She sat back against the couch and her gaze connected once more. "Ah, yes. Your waiver." She sipped at her coffee. "Though such a document isn't necessary, if it will make you feel more comfortable, then by all means have it drawn up. I'll accept it."

Relaxation seeped into her tense body for the first time since she'd looked out her dormer window. The feeling was short-lived.

"What I won't accept is leaving it at that, as you put it. It won't matter that you aren't making a claim, Megan. Before I left the farm this morning, I contacted my own attorney. I had him begin the process of settling your inheritance on you."

The cup and saucer she'd just lifted clattered to the table. "I don't want your money."

"Be that as it may." Elizabeth's eyes were shrewd and determined. "It will be done. And it's not my money. It's yours, set aside long ago for any descendants of my daughter, Anne. My attorney will also be addressing the change of circumstances in my will."

Meggy shot a harried look at Shan, who shrugged. Though Elizabeth couldn't quite be considered the fire-breathing she-dragon she'd feared finding, she wasn't the warm and fuzzy, cookie-baking type of grandmother she'd hoped for either. No, Elizabeth Ashford was a steam roller in pearls. Meggy had rolled over her share of timid souls these past years and considered her assertiveness a positive trait.

But could the pushy matriarch accept her for who and what she was, or would she insist on molding her into some sort of perfect, society doll? The possibility made her palms sweat. "You don't know for sure I'm Rachel's daughter," she insisted. "It could all be a big misunderstanding. This DNA test you mentioned? What if I refuse to have it done?"

"You're grasping at straws, Megan." Elizabeth leaned forward, setting her coffee on the table. When she met her gaze, the shrewdness had faded from her eyes, to be replaced with a gentle compassion. "You have nothing to fear from me, from us. I've been looking for you for over a quarter century. The moment I saw you at the farm, I knew you were mine. I don't need a test to confirm it."

Meggy didn't know what to say to that, didn't think she could say anything around the lump in her throat. *I'm hers?*

Elizabeth sat back. "Now that the tedious financial concerns have been dealt with, we can get to the personal ones. I know you must have questions, but I'm an old lady, so humor me."

The twinkle in her eyes was anything but old.

"I want to know everything about you. So, start at the beginning."

She could only stare wide-eyed at the tiny dynamo perched across from her. Nothing was settled as far as she was concerned, but she couldn't help but be charmed by the woman's impish smile. They'd see about the money, in the meantime, she found she couldn't resist the possibilities shining in Elizabeth Ashford's eyes.

Meggy extended Rachel's letter across the table. "Perhaps we should start with this."

## Chapter Seventeen

Meggy slipped the buttons on her smock, letting it slide from her weary shoulders with an appreciative sigh. It joined the slacks on the floor at the foot of her bed. In bra and panties, she headed for the refrigerator and a bottle of water.

She wandered to the tiny dormer window overlooking the driveway. Popping the cap on the bottle, she took a long swig while staring down at the dimly lit carriage house. Muted light shown from the windows, illuminating the large black Mercedes parked just outside. A large shadow moved past one of the windows, and she took a step backward before catching herself. When she realized what she'd done, she snorted in self-disgust.

The shadow shifted once more, and she made herself turn away. Their deceitful tenant was still awake, despite the lateness of the hour. She hoped something he'd eaten had disagreed with him. It would serve him right. Then she rolled her eyes. Since he'd eaten dinner in the Palmer House lounge, he'd probably sue her. He was a lawyer, licensed in Massachusetts, after all.

*The bastard.* A low growl escaped her throat as she sat on the edge of the bed. She set the water bottle on the nightstand before dropping to her back to stare at the ceiling.

He'd worn a satisfied smile when he'd returned to

escort Elizabeth to her rooms at The Palmerton Inn. Considering the reception he'd received only an hour earlier, she hadn't seen what he had to smile about. Well, other than the fact that her demand he vacate the carriage house had no teeth and they both knew it. Why he would want to continue the lease when he'd already gotten what he'd come for was a mystery. But she'd been too emotionally exhausted and heartsick to analyze his motives.

She'd immersed herself in the many details involved in running a smooth kitchen, and by the time the dinner crowd began to arrive, she'd managed to relax. The dozens of times Trevor's betrayal had intruded on her peace, she'd forced the anguish to a dark corner of her mind and concentrated on what she *could* control. Producing a fabulous dining experience for her customers.

Mentally patting herself on the back for a job well done, she'd stepped into the dining room for her nightly appearance. Her composure shattered when she spotted the reason for her disquiet seated at his usual spot at the bar.

From the sour look on Shan's face, her devoted friend wasn't any happier with his presence than she. Shan's mouth was pulled in a tight line as she set a draft beer in front of Jasper, perched on the stool beside Trevor. The hush that went through the unusually large number of locals in the lounge continued while Meggy completed her turn around the dining room.

She couldn't recall a single word she'd said to the diners. For all she knew, she'd babbled like an idiot. All of her concentration was focused on denying the urge to march up to the bar and knock the billionaire lawyer on his ass.

Seeing him sitting so chummily with Jasper, her throat closed up at the realization that there would be still more unpleasant fallout to face from yesterday's revelations. Just a matter of time until the whole town knew the truth. That truth being, the Palmerton pit bull had made a complete and utter fool of herself, lapping up Trevor's deceitful attention like a desperate pound puppy while the entire town looked on.

Until very recently, she hadn't been one to run from an unpleasant situation. Facing things head-on had always been her style. It pissed her off that she wanted to run, from *him*, so she focused on the anger instead. She'd be damned if she'd let him intimidate her in her own place.

She lifted her chin against the curious looks that followed her as she approached the bar. There'd be no more embarrassing shows for the town's entertainment. Until Trevor took her words to heart and went away, she would simply ignore him.

Shan's gaze was full of impotent apology.

Meggy did her best to reassure her friend with a smile. She ignored Trevor's disturbing presence, focusing her attention on Jasper. "Hello, Jasper." She paused beside his stool. "If I'd known you were coming in tonight, I would have added my sour cream pumpkin cake to the menu," she said, knowing of his notorious sweet tooth and of his enjoyment of that recipe in particular.

"I hadn't planned to come in tonight," the town's oldest citizen admitted. "But after this afternoon's excitement..." He chuckled and his eyes twinkled. "I decided to come check out things for myself."

"This afternoon's excitement?"

The old man fixed her with a stare, the knowing look in his eyes telling her he was well aware she was consciously avoiding looking at the man sitting to his right. His gaze shrewd, he turned to pin Trevor with a glittering smile. "It looks like you've got some more groveling to do if you're going to get back in her good graces."

"Excuse me?" She blinked, at a loss. No one but the O'Sheas knew there was a reason for Trevor to have fallen out of her good graces. None of *them* would have shared her shame.

"The writer here." Jasper jerked his head in Trevor's direction. "Who, it turns out is no writer at all, came into the Bluebell today to explain his real reasons for coming to town."

"He what?" She finally looked at Trevor. Her fingers curled into claws at the crooked smile on his face. "You what?"

"They would have found out the truth soon, anyway. I just made sure they got the correct story. And I wanted to apologize for being dishonest with everyone."

Jasper ignored her gasp at Trevor's calm explanation. "I admit I was none too happy to learn he'd lied, but once he'd explained the situation, it was easy to see it from his point of view. Imagine, our own little Meggy, the long lost heir to the Ashford fortune. Why, it's like something you'd read about in a book." He cackled a dry laugh. "Besides, I owed him one for all those meals he bought me."

Jasper's endorsement was one shock too many, in a day full of incomprehensible shocks. She flew at Trevor, her eyes blazing. She forgot where she was and the avid audience. Shan was already skirting the edge of the bar in an attempt to head off the explosion when it hit.

She shoved him for all she was worth, disappointed when he barely budged on the stool, which shouldn't have surprised her. He had ten inches and fifty pounds on her. Still, it infuriated her that he wasn't laying flat out on the floor.

Instead, he rose to his feet and reached out a hand.

She slapped it away. "You announced my private business in front of the entire crowd at the Bluebell?" She gulped in air. "You had no right!"

The commotion had caught the attention of not just those in the lounge. Quiet had descended over the dining room as well.

The oddity of that had brought a curious Cal out of the kitchen. He hurried toward the bar at Shan's pleading look.

"You had no right!" Meggy repeated on a shout.

However Trevor would have responded was lost when Cal stepped between them. Her sous chef slung a thick arm over her trembling shoulders and began muscling her toward the kitchen, calling out in false cheerfulness, "You're needed in the kitchen, boss." He leaned close to press his mouth to her ear. "Meg, are you crazy? The entire place is watching and listening."

Hours later, she was still horrified that she'd let loose her temper without a single thought for her customers. The man was making her crazy! She flicked off the lamp and stared at the dark shadows on the ceiling of her quiet room.

The only good thing that had happened on this day from hell had been her conversation with her great-grandmother. Surprisingly, she'd been left hopeful they could eventually forge a mutually satisfying relationship. Far from slamming the proverbial door in her face, Elizabeth was demanding they get to know one another—and amazingly was staying in town to see that happened. To her delight, she found the Ashford matriarch to be a charmingly assertive woman. A tough old bird with a soft heart, as Brody had described her. She smiled at the apt description.

That soft heart had been apparent in the tears she'd shed when she'd read Rachel's letter. She'd gone on to tell her what she believed had led to Rachel's disappearance all those years ago and her subsequent decision to give up an unexpected baby. Rachel had always been a difficult child, she'd explained, wanting her freedom from the time she was eleven or so. She'd never shouldered responsibilities well, especially those that came along with the Ashford name. She had bristled against the need for the security being Anne's daughter required, even when she was very young. Elizabeth suspected she'd begun using drugs, perhaps in rebellion, but that was just assumption. Whatever the reason, she'd been an unhappy young woman.

The postal stamp on Rachel's letter was the first real lead they'd had on her whereabouts in a quarter century. Meggy had seen the hopeful excitement in Elizabeth's eyes, even as she admitted that if Rachel still didn't want to be found, the odds of doing so weren't good. The letter had been written four years ago and, for Elizabeth's sake, Meggy could only hope it wasn't another dead end. She couldn't give Elizabeth back her granddaughter, but she *could* settle the matter of her great-granddaughter. First thing tomorrow, she'd have the DNA test done.

Shutting her eyes, she tried to will herself to sleep, but her mind insisted on playing a film strip of memories against her closed eyelids. She told herself to focus on the fury that had blasted from Trevor's pale eyes when she'd slipped off his charm bracelet, but those other, softer images kept sliding back in to thrash and tear at her. Trevor's smile that first morning in the carriage house. His boyish excitement at the unexpected treat of floor seats for the Celtics game. His seeming sincerity as he held out a fat, silver heart and told her he loved her.

Fighting against the silent stream of salty tears flowing into her hairline, she squeezed her eyelids tight.

She'd been a fool, scoffing at women she'd met over the years who yearned for a man who'd crushed their hearts under a careless heel. But she hadn't understood. Hadn't known the true scope of her woman's heart. Hadn't realized that once given, once caressed by the fingers of love, that tender organ pulsed with a steadfast beat that transcended pain, and betrayal, and the knowledge of the mind.

Trevor Bryce Christos, with his dimpled smiles and calculated deceit, wasn't worthy of a single thought, much less her heart. Her mind railed at the injustice of his betrayal, demanding she cross him off as a difficult, but well-learned lesson, but her heart... Her heart lay shattered in a thousand razor sharp shards.

With a low moan, she rolled to her side and curled in a tight ball. Her gasping sobs echoed in the silence, an audible witness to the painful quaking of her grieving mind and body.

## Chapter Eighteen

Trevor flung open the door to the carriage house and scowled at the empty driveway. *Where the hell had she gone?* The question had been driving him crazy since he'd watched her climb into the big SUV that had rumbled up the driveway a few minutes before seven that morning.

Justin Cooper had hopped out of the vehicle and strolled through the front door of Palmer House as though he had every right to be there. He'd emerged several moments later, his arm slung across the shoulders of a smiling Meggy.

The door slammed with a satisfying thump. He wasn't accustomed to leaving a pressing situation hanging as he had with Meggy, any more than he was accustomed to having a woman who claimed to love him refuse to speak to him—unless it was to yell at him. A number of women had claimed to love him over the years, and each of *them* had done everything they could to get close to him and stay there. Now that he had finally found the one woman he *wanted* close, she didn't want anything to do with him. The situation was unacceptable and infuriating.

And his fault, he knew.

The knowledge didn't make it easier to accept. Not that he was accepting anything. This situation couldn't be allowed to go on indefinitely. He had no intention of letting her call a halt to their relationship as she planned.

In the meantime, he was needed in Virginia. A problem at one of the family's holdings needed his immediate attention. He forked fingers through his hair. And Meggy and Elizabeth needed some time to get to know each other. They could have the time until he returned, and then, by damn, he and Meggy would have things out. He paced the room once more just as he'd done so many times during the night.

Her relationship with Justin Cooper would be the first thing they addressed. He wasn't about to stand by and let some muscle-bound cop beat his time.

The sound of a vehicle turning up the drive had him rushing to the door. He yanked it open just as a black pickup truck came to a stop at the back of Palmer House.

Cara Finnegan's curvy frame slid from the lifted vehicle to land gracefully on the ground.

With the sharp claws of jealousy shredding his already tenuous control, he stomped up the walkway. He didn't wait for her to finish pulling the two shopping bags from the cab of the truck. He leaned past her and grabbed them himself.

She yelped at his unexpected presence.

"Where's Meggy?" he demanded.

"Do you always sneak up on people and scare the crap out of them?" She snatched the bags from his hands. "Or am I just today's lucky victim of your inconsiderate tendencies?"

"I'm sorry," he grumbled, and he was. He knew his temper was a bad one, and Meggy's best friend was the last person he wanted to alienate. "I didn't mean to frighten you. I just thought you'd know where Meggy ran off to."

"Aren't you the clever one?" Her big green eyes sparkled like cold emeralds and her voice was a slicing purr. "It just so happens I *do* know where Meggy ran off to, but I wouldn't tell you, even if you offered me, oh, let's say...three quarters of a billion dollars!"

"Cara." He sighed, his shoulders slumping. "I know the way I handled things looks bad, but…"

"Bad?" Fury was evident in the stiffening of every curvy inch of her body. "What you did stinks! I don't like what you did, and if we're being truthful here, I don't think I like you either!"

"I was protecting my grandmother, Cara. And Meggy isn't completely innocent in this situation. If she'd come to the farm and been honest with us, none of this would have happened."

"She didn't go down there, lie to you, and make you fall in love with her, you son of a bitch."

"No, she didn't. But she wasn't the only one to fall in love. Do you know how difficult it is to discover you've fallen in love with someone you consider a thief? Believe me, that wasn't in my plans."

One of the shopping bags slid to the crook of an elbow when she lifted her hand to her temple, rubbing. "You hurt her," she growled.

He took a step closer. "I hurt her. I did. I'm sorry about that, and I'll make it up to her as soon as she calms down enough to let me close again. I love her, Cara, and I mean to marry her."

A frown appeared on her stunning face, and she blinked suddenly. She braced her free hand against the truck beside them, the contents of the second bag thudded against the driver's door. "If you used that silver tongue on her, I can see why she fell in love with you."

Her unexpected acknowledgement of Meggy's feelings eased some of his panic. "She told you she loves me, huh?"

The frown turned to a scowl. "That's your one freebie, Trevor. If you hurt her again...well, you won't like the consequences. She's special to me."

"She's special to me, too. If I can ever get her to calm down and talk to me, I'll prove that." A thought occurred, and his gaze sharpened. "She seems as scared as she is mad. Do you have any idea why that would be so?"

"You already had your freebie, Trevor. Don't push it."

"Cara, I can't fix things with her if I don't understand the problem."

She stared at him.

He could see her loyalty to her friend bumping up against her desire to help.

The fingers of one hand continued to rub at her temple. Finally, she sighed. "Did you know that after going to the farm, she couldn't decide if she really wanted to make contact with Elizabeth?"

"Why?"

"The money. It scared her."

Her answer made no sense. "Again, why?"

"She believes that kind of money warps people. She couldn't understand why Rachel would choose adoption over going to her family for help and figured Elizabeth must have been the problem." She glanced up at the main house. "Palmer House is her dream, Trevor, a dream she's been working for her whole life. She won't let anyone endanger that. With the resources at her disposal, Elizabeth Ashford could destroy that dream."

Trevor would have scoffed at that, but she'd suddenly gone sheet white. "Hey, are you okay?"

She nodded, but then she swayed and her voice grew garbled. "Oh, hell."

"Shit!"

He caught her just before she hit the ground. Completely limp, with the bulging shopping bags dragging at her arms, she threw him off balance. He landed on his ass right there in the driveway, doing his best to cradle her in his lap.

His heart in his throat, he patted her face, with no results. His gaze darted about in search of help, finding none. "Don't do this to me." He patted her face again and jumped at the ring of a phone coming from the purse still draped over one of her shoulders. It took some doing, but he finally managed to free both the purse and the shopping bag from her arm. Fishing out the phone, he jabbed at the button to connect.

"Oh, thank God," he said to the unknown caller.

A moment of silence ensued. "Who is this?"

"It's Trevor Christos." He patted Cara's face again.

"Why the hell are you answering my wife's phone?"

"Finn?" He was too rattled to soften the blow. "Finn, you're wife just fainted."

"What?" Finn's bark exploded through the phone.

"Jesus. She went down like a ton of bricks!" He knew he sounded panicked, but he couldn't help it.

"Where are you?"

"I'm sitting on my ass in the driveway of Palmer House."

"I'll be there in two minutes."

"Make it one," Trevor said to the dead line. "Cara, honey," he crooned after tossing aside the phone and freeing her other arm of the remaining bag. "Come on, sweetheart, don't do this to me." In the past three days he'd had two women faint on him. He never wanted to experience the phenomenon again.

The sound of a vehicle turning into the driveway made him almost giddy with relief. He forgot all about wanting to strangle the man when Justin Cooper's big SUV rumbled up the drive. Help had arrived and that was all that mattered. Gesturing frantically, he beckoned to Meggy and Justin as they scrambled out of the vehicle.

"Cara!" Meggy dropped to her knees beside him. Her wild eyes met his. "What did you do to her?"

"I didn't do anything to her. She fainted."

"You must have done something." She pressed her palm to Cara's pale cheek.

Justin crouched beside them and pressed a finger to Cara's neck. "Have you called nine-one-one?"

Trevor shook his head. He hadn't even thought to. "Finn called a minute ago. He's on his way." He looked around for the phone he'd dropped. "Her phone is there, Meggy. Call nine-one-one," he said a little desperately.

She didn't get the chance. Before she could scramble to retrieve Cara's phone, squealing tires roared up the driveway.

The luxury car was still rocking from the sudden stop when Finn vaulted from the driver's door and skidded to a stop on his knees at Cara's side. He looked as pale as his wife. "Baby." He bent to brush his cheek against hers. "Baby, you're scaring the shit out of everyone. Wake up."

When her eyelids fluttered open, four sets of lungs breathed a collective sigh of relief. Her gaze fastened on Finn's. "I fainted." She blinked at him.

Finn met her confused frown with a relieved smile. "And took a year off my life in the process." He looked at Trevor, who cradled Cara in his arms as gently as if she were made of spun glass. His laughter was a deep rumble. "From the look on his face, I'd say you cost Trevor at least a decade."

Cara tilted her head back to look up into Trevor's sweating face. Her smile was wry. "Sorry about that, Trevor. Thanks for catching me."

"My pleasure." He attempted a smile and failed. "But if you decide to do this again, do me a favor and call someone else."

She chuckled.

Meggy leaned over her. "God, Cara, do me a favor, and don't do this again at *all*." She looked at Finn. "Should I call nine-one-one?"

He shook his head. "No. Let's just get her inside." He scooped her from Trevor's arms and stood as though she weighed no more than a child.

Meggy scrambled to her feet, hurrying ahead of them to open the front door.

Justin swept up the shopping bags and held out a hand. "Women."

Trevor took the hand offered and rose to his feet, agreeing with the sentiment completely.

Finn had settled Cara on one of the couches in the lounge when Trevor and Justin walked inside.

At the bar, Meggy filled a glass with cool water, rushing to the couch to shove it into Cara's hands.

"What happened?"

Cara sipped at the glass, but kept her eyes on Finn as he settled his hip on the edge of the couch and brushed at the dark curls at her temple.

Meggy rounded on Trevor. "What did you do? You must have said something to upset her."

Trevor understood her anxiety, but he was getting pretty damned tired of being the bad guy in her mind. He opened his mouth to tell her exactly what they had been discussing.

"He didn't do anything, Meggy." Cara spoke from the couch. Her gaze met Finn's, and she smiled when he nodded. "I fainted because I'm pregnant. We've known for a few weeks, but we'd planned to wait a little while before making the announcement." Her smile was luminous. "I'm going to have a baby, Meggy."

"Oh, Cara." She laughed and shot Finn a smart-ass grin. "I'm impressed. I didn't think you had it in you."

Finn smiled, his gaze on his wife. It was obvious nothing could shake his self-satisfaction at the moment.

Meggy insisted on popping open a bottle of champagne to celebrate the news. Cara insisted on water.

Ten minutes passed before Finn helped his wife to her feet and escorted her to the car. He'd send someone by later to collect the pickup, he said. Justin left close on their heels, but not close enough for Trevor, especially when he stopped at the door to sweep Meggy into his arms.

Grinning at him over Meggy's shoulder, he dipped his head to give her a smacking kiss on the mouth. "You know where to find me if you need me."

Trevor's hands curled into fists.

"I always do," she answered with a smile in her voice. "Thanks for today."

"My pleasure, babe."

He left chuckling.

Chapter Nineteen

"Where the hell have you been for the last three hours?" Trevor demanded the moment the door closed behind Justin. "And just what is Justin Cooper to you?"

Meggy stepped to the coffee table and bent to gather the empty glasses. Justin was shocked and amused upon hearing the details surrounding her surprising connection to Elizabeth Ashford and had insisted on taking her to breakfast so that he could grill her properly. She'd dragged him along to the lab for the DNA test afterward.

And she'd be damned if she would explain any of that to Trevor Christos.

"The answer to both of those questions is, none of your business."

She didn't hear him move, but suddenly his arm clamped around her belly from behind, and she found herself hauled up against a very solid body. The glasses she'd been gathering clinked against each other in her fingers.

"Think again, Meggy," he growled in her ear. "Everything about you has been my business since you gave yourself to me that first night."

His chest expanded on a breath at her back and despite her anger, she felt the rush of heat the contact produced in her body.

"I told you there'd be no going back once that door

was shut, and you agreed. I meant every word."

She struggled against his grip, to no avail. His arms remained around her, and when she couldn't free herself she went still, lashing out with the only weapon available to her. "You haven't meant a word you've said from the moment you arrived in Palmerton." She started to struggle again. His breath heated her temple where he pressed his face to hers.

"Stop, baby." His tone lost the edge of anger to come out a gentle purr. "You're going to hurt yourself."

"Let me go, and I'll be fine."

In a gesture of weariness that was so unlike him, his forehead dropped to her shoulder. "I can't."

The longing in his voice was palpable, and she struggled against the urge to turn in his arms and pull him close in comfort. He's a liar and a manipulator, she reminded her weakening heart. "You mean you *won't*," she corrected. She suppressed a shudder when his cheek brushed against hers.

"You accepted my heart, Meggy. Taking off my bracelet doesn't change that. Can't or won't. I'm not going to let you go."

"You never had me in the first place."

His arms tightened about her, telegraphing his returning anger at her denial. "I had you, Meggy. I've had you in just about every way a man can have a woman."

She stiffened, which should have given him warning. The back of her head connected with his chin when she threw it back.

"Ouch! Damn it, that hurt."

She jerked from his loosened arms. Spinning on him, she glared as he rubbed at his chin. "That wasn't you who had me. That was a writer named Trevor Bryce. We both know *he* doesn't exist."

It was fascinating, really, the way he physically expanded with fury. His hand dropped slowly and his chest rose on a slow, measured breath. His eyes blazed. She half expected his thick pelt of hair to stand on end. Her eyes widened at the sight, and she barely stopped herself from stepping back in defense.

"That's bullshit, and we both know it."

His voice was soft with menace and when he dipped his head closer, she *did* step back. He followed until they were nose to nose.

"It was *my* love you demanded that night on Christos' Chariot. *Mine!* And it was *my* heart you accepted. Whether my last name is Bryce or Christos, it doesn't matter. The person you said you loved was me."

The truth of his statement ate at her pride like acid, and her own temper flared. "You lied to me."

"You said you loved me," he pressed, his eyes hot with frustration. "Were you lying?"

She forced herself to take a calming breath and held her ground. "Don't turn this back on me. You're the liar here." He looked so disappointed that she felt a lash of guilt. He'd lied to her. How dare he look disappointed when she called him on it?

"Yes, I lied. As did you, coming to the farm under the pretense of looking for a position. I did what needed to be done to protect Elizabeth, and I've apologized. Though I'd do it again if I thought such action was necessary." He shoved a hand through his hair, further messing his already mussed locks. "I don't understand what's got you so scared, but I meant every word I said that night. I love you. If you think I'll let you go after you admitted loving me in return, you don't know me at all."

His words should have thrilled her, did thrill her if she was being honest with herself, but he was right. She *was* scared. She was terrified because she *didn't* know him. She'd thought she had, but that had been when he was a simple, though wealthy, writer. The billionaire lawyer who stood before her, bristling with anger, was a stranger. One she didn't trust.

Lifting her chin, she met his intense gaze. "You're right, I don't know you. I fell in love with a charming man who doesn't exist. In his place, I found a cynical, distrustful man, willing to play the romantic to get what he wants. My love was an illusion, just...like...you."

Reaching out, he pinched her chin between thumb and index finger. He didn't hurt her, but he held her firm when she tried to jerk away. "The only illusion around here is yours, thinking I'll let you go. You know me, Meggy, and you're right. I *will* do what I have to, to get what I want."

She didn't fight him when he lifted her face until he could close his mouth over hers. She couldn't. Even now, when her pride demanded she find some satisfying uses for Cara's machete, she found the taste and feel of his mouth moving over hers irresistible. She knew she should fight the wild response her body clamored to give him. Instead, she felt herself falling headlong into the swirling heat branding her as his. Helplessly, she pressed close to the hard angles of his body.

His tongue sank deep, taking her mouth in a thorough claiming before he lifted his head. Smoky gray eyes glittered with satisfaction as they smoldered inches from hers.

"Whatever it takes. Remember that." Stepping back, he set her free. "I have some business to attend to in Virginia. It'll take me the better part of a week. That's all the time I'll give you to get over your anger. When I get back, we'll settle this once and for all." He turned and walked out the door.

\*\*\*\*

"Nobody tells me anything!" Erin burst into Shan's kitchen with a pout pulling at her lips.

"Bitch. Bitch. Bitch." Cara met her frown with a grin.

Meggy said nothing, sipping at her iced-tea. Her day had already been a long one, the meeting with her parents this morning embarrassing and exhausting. They were hurt and concerned, not understanding why she hadn't informed them of what had been happening in her life.

She'd put their concerns involving Elizabeth to rest at least. Her feelings for Trevor were more difficult to explain. She'd ended up giving them a carefully edited version of events. Hours later, it still bothered her that, when filtered through all the facts, he hadn't come across as quite the bastard she'd named him.

Erin harrumphed, bringing her attention back to the present. "I shouldn't have to stop by the Bluebell to find out what's going on with my own family."

"Like what?" Shan set a pitcher of iced tea on the table and sat.

Cara smiled into her water glass.

Meggy just shrugged. It wasn't her place to tell Cara's sisters they were going to be aunts. Still, she wondered how the grapevine had gotten wind of it so fast.

Erin slumped into the last open chair and glared at her in silence.

"Why are you looking at me? I just found out myself."

"You just found out?" Erin parroted. "Please!"

"We weren't going to say anything just yet," Cara interjected. "The only reason we told Meggy is because she was there when I fainted."

"You fainted?" Concern flooded Shan's eyes.

"Well, yeah. But I'm fine. My doctor says that's not uncommon in the first trimester."

"First trimester? You're pregnant?" Erin squealed with surprised delight. Cara nodded, wearing a wide smile. Shan, with her soft heart, covered her sister's hand. It took the O'Shea sisters a full five minutes to deal with their excitement.

When their celebration had cooled down to simple pleasure, she questioned Erin. "What was it you learned at the Bluebell, if it wasn't about Cara being pregnant?"

"I heard about your engagement to Trevor. I'm pissed you didn't tell me yourself."

"Her what?" Cara sputtered.

Shan's brows rose and she studied Meggy. "You're engaged? I thought you were mad at him."

"I am. Mad at him, I mean." She scowled at Erin. "Who said we were engaged?"

"Everyone." Erin looked confused. "Aren't you?"

*He wouldn't.*

"If I am," Meggy said slowly, "it's the first I've heard of it."

"Well, Clara Watson told me she'd heard it straight from Trevor."

*It was obvious he would.* She dropped her head to

the table.

"Hmmm," Shan hummed into her iced tea.

"Wait." Erin held up a hand. "Why would he tell Clara you're engaged if you're not?"

She groaned without lifting her head. "Because he's the devil."

Cara snickered. "Sounds like the man is attempting an end run around you, Meggy."

She sat up. "Well, he's about to be called offside."

"Are you saying he hasn't actually asked you to marry him?" Erin's wide eyes betrayed her shock.

"That's what I'm saying." She got up to walk to the window and stood staring out at the empty carriage house below. With him off to Virginia, she'd been looking forward to a little peace. She never dreamed he'd do something so...Machiavellian before he left. She should have. Devious methods seemed to be the way he operated.

"That's diabolical," Erin murmured, "and a little bit romantic too," she added after a moment's pause.

Meggy scowled over her shoulder. "You had it right the first time."

Cara met her gaze. "You have to admit, a guy that determined to have a woman is hard to resist."

Meggy choked back a snort. If she'd done a better job of resisting the jerk, she wouldn't be the current target for the gossiping busybodies down at the Blue Bell. She cringed inwardly. The gall of the man. When she saw him again... The thought sent tingles of something suspiciously like excitement racing over her skin and left goose bumps behind.

*Stop right there, missy. You don't* ever *want to see him again. Remember?*

She pivoted to lean her hips against the counter. "I thought you were mad at him. What happened to your plan to use a machete on certain portions of his anatomy?"

"I never planned to use it on *him*, just his stuff." Cara grinned. "And I *am* still mad at him. I'm just not pissed anymore."

"Why not?" Meggy wanted to know. "This is just another example of the way he works. He's sneaky and deceitful."

"And let's not forget determined." Erin ignored her glare.

"Actually," Shan said before she could respond, "a sneaky man wouldn't have announced his intentions to the entire town."

"Which leaves deceitful." Cara cocked her head in thought. "And a truly deceitful man wouldn't have gone to the Bluebell to apologize. As much as I'd like to attribute that particularly nasty trait to the man, I can't in this case. Especially not after he told me himself that he plans to marry you."

"What?" She shot out of her slouch against the counter. "When was this?"

"Yesterday. Right before I fainted." Cara waved a dismissive hand. "The sticking point for me is you told me yourself you'd expected him to ask you to marry him and that your answer would be yes when he did."

The reminder pierced her heart in a bull's-eye, causing a fresh flow of grief to seep from the open wound. She'd dreamed of spending a lifetime full of love and laughter with a sexy, thoughtful man, but the dream had become nightmare. The teasing author who'd stolen her heart was as fictitious as their supposed engagement. "That was before he turned out to be a liar...and a lawyer!" She dumped the dregs of her iced tea into the sink and set it down with a thump. "What's with the three of you? I thought you were on *my* side!"

"We are," they said in unison.

"Doesn't feel like it." She crossed her arms over her chest and frowned.

Shan leaned on her elbows. "Do you still love him, Meggy?"

"That's beside the point. I don't trust him."

Cara shook her head. "No, that is exactly the point. And your lack of trust is *his* problem, and he'll have to fix that. But something he said to me yesterday made me consider his behavior through a different lens."

Meggy's mouth flattened in a frown when Cara didn't elaborate. "Well, don't stop there, Oprah. Enlighten us."

Cara grinned. "He asked me if I knew how difficult it was to discover you'd fallen in love with someone you believed to be a thief."

That warm and mushy feeling bubbled up in her belly at hearing he'd fallen in love with her, even before he'd discovered her innocence. It was no use. Despite his latest sneaky maneuver, she was still in love with him. She felt like crying.

"God knows the two of you have some major issues to sort through," Cara continued, watching her, "but the bottom line is you love him, and if he's to be believed, he loves you too." She laughed. "It takes balls to stroll into the Bluebell and make your intentions the number one topic on the grapevine. Are you really letting a guy like that get away?"

Was she? Only time would tell if putting her

feelings for Trevor behind her was even possible, and if the last forty-eight hours were any indication, the process would be long and painful. Besides, she didn't like the woman she'd become since the moment she'd read Rachel's letter. The *real* Meggy Calhoun met challenges head on. So why was she backing down from the most important challenge of her life?

Trevor wasn't the only one who'd been pretending to be something he wasn't. Time he met the *real* Palmerton pit bull. She loved him, damn it, and he claimed to love her. Well, then, it was time he proved it.

She pushed herself away from the counter. "I've got to get down to the kitchen. Erin, could you help me put together a costume for next week's Halloween party?"

At the sudden change in topic, the sisters looked at each other in confusion.

"For you?" Erin sat up in her chair. "I thought you said you weren't dressing up?"

"I've changed my mind." She bared her teeth in a sharp smile.

"I know that look." Cara's eyes narrowed. "What are you planning?"

"A little revenge."

Cara leaned forward. "Operation payback. I like the sound of that. What are you going to do?"

"Make him miserable."

"You go, girl!" Shan laughed.

"And I'm taking a page right out of his sneaky playbook to do it." Thoughts danced through her mind. Devious thoughts. And she welcomed them. "He's not the only one who can plant ideas on the town grapevine."

Cara grinned. "Poor Trevor. I almost feel sorry for

him."

She raised a brow. "He says he loves me. I'm making him prove it."

"But are you going to forgive him?"

She headed for the stairs, calling over her shoulder, "I guess I'll have to, since I've decided I'm marrying him."

"Wait a minute," Cara sputtered. "You can't just drop a bomb like that and then walk away. I want details!"

"I'll fill you in on the details as soon as I figure them out." She hit the stairs, flipping open her cell phone. "Hey, babe," she said as she descended the stairs to the kitchen, "I need a little more help."

Chapter Twenty

"I heard an interesting bit of gossip over at the Bluebell this morning."

"You don't say?"

Brody sipped coffee, his hips propped against a counter, while Meggy labored at the prep table with a wickedly sharp chopping knife. Since Trevor's departure a week earlier, the bulky bodyguard had practically taken up residence at Palmer House and his hovering presented a number of opportunities to further her plan for revenge.

She'd discarded her original horrified suspicion that as the Ashford heir, she needed protection, and Trevor had assigned Brody the task. Instead, she suspected he was there simply to keep Trevor informed of the goings on in Palmerton, specifically, her own. That sly state of affairs suited her fine. In fact, she appreciated Brody's assistance in keeping Trevor informed of her actions, particularly since Brody appeared to be so uncomfortable with the chore.

It was charming really, the way he had taken it upon himself to assist her in overcoming her anger by plying her with anecdotal glimpses into Trevor's childhood. Still, she felt no remorse using the mountainous menace. He'd brought up the idea himself, after all, that day on the ferry when he suggested she gain a little revenge before she forgave Trevor.

Out of the corner of her eye, she saw him finger aside the airline voucher she'd purposefully left out on the counter, to read the name of the local medical lab on the envelope beneath it. The envelope contained the paperwork from the DNA test she'd taken last week, but he wouldn't know that. She wasn't surprised when he didn't comment on either and knew he'd be on the phone with Trevor within the hour.

"The good citizens of Palmerton have a pool going," he said instead.

"There's always some kind of pool going on over at the Bluebell. The practice is a favorite local pastime."

"Don't you want to know what they're betting on?"

"The suspense is killing me," she drawled without looking at him. "Tell me quick."

Brody chuckled at her dry tone. "The locals are choosing sides on who will win the heart of the Palmerton pit bull. Will it be the billionaire lawyer, who just last week announced his engagement to the lady, or the charming cop who's been seen escorting the sexy chef on several occasions over the last few days?"

"Who's showing the best odds?" She kept her tone light, as though the entire town discussing her love life made no difference.

"Considering your temper and the fact that you let it be known you hadn't been informed of Trevor's fictitious proposal, not to mention all those mysterious outings you and the cop have disappeared on lately, the locals give the cop a slight lead." Beefy arms crossed over his broad chest. "My money is on Trevor."

She shrugged. "It's your checkbook."

He shook his head. "I hope you know what you're doing, Meggy. Trevor isn't a man to cross."

"I'm a grown woman, perfectly capable of choosing who I spend time with. Trevor can rant and rave all he wants. I'll see who I want, when I want."

"You're saying your sudden interest in the cop is legit?"

"Did I say that?"

"That's what it sounded like."

"You're awfully interested in my love life, Brody. Living vicariously?"

He looked thoughtful for a moment. "Trevor can be a real bastard when someone messes with what he considers his. And don't fool yourself, Meggy, in Trevor's mind, you're his. I'm just looking out for your interests."

"So am I."

"By trying to make Trevor jealous with the cop?" He indicated the envelopes beside him on the counter with a nod of his head. "You're playing with fire, lady."

"Who said I'm trying to make Trevor jealous? I happen to love Justin."

"Since when? According to Trevor, you claimed you were in love with *him* only last week."

"And last week he claimed he was a simple writer." She felt her temper leaking through the calm she'd worked to achieve. She took a steadying breath but kept up the rhythmic thwacking of the knife on the cutting board. "I've known Justin for years and loved him almost as long, but more importantly, he's never lied to me."

Up to that point, Brody had appeared merely amused by her answers. The worried frown that slipped across his battered features told her she'd begun to make him nervous. "Jesus, Meggy. Trevor's in love with you.

You don't think he's going to just step aside and let you fly off with this guy, do you?"

The knife stilled in her hand. "If I decide to fly off with this guy, as you put it, he'll have no other choice." Despite her decision to take Trevor at his word—after she exacted a little revenge—his betrayal still hurt. It wasn't necessary to feign anger, she knew her eyes glittered with it. "Drop it, Brody. The topic just pisses me off." She flipped the knife over to scrape sliced mushrooms into a holding tray. "So, have you found a costume yet for the party tomorrow night? My great-grandmother is coming as Queen Elizabeth." Her eyes narrowed on a sneer. "You could come as her jester."

\*\*\*\*

The Halloween bash had been in full swing for several hours. Meggy glanced out the window toward the carriage house for what felt like the hundredth time. She forced herself to look away. He wasn't coming. He certainly hadn't raced home to stop her from running off to marry Justin. Either he didn't believe she'd do it or he didn't care. The latter possibility made her want to weep.

When her parents waltzed by on the makeshift dance floor, she pasted a smile on her face. Bob and Carol Calhoun looked so easy together, the balding fifties biker and his poodle-skirted date. A pang of sadness tugged at her heart that she'd never experience the kind of love they shared, and she blamed Trevor. He'd made her want things she'd never known she wanted and then he'd turned out to be a liar. She didn't know why she still wanted the bastard.

"Any sign of the billionaire lawyer?" Justin, in his rock star's garb, slung an arm around her shoulders, his gaze scanning the crowd of partiers. He was careful not to disturb the glittered wings on her fairy costume, which he'd told her was sexy as hell and was going to have Trevor choking on his own tongue.

She wished now that she'd worn her chef's smock.

At the bar, her gypsy earrings sparkling in the overhead lights, Cara shook her head. Finn, her six-five gypsy prince, leaned on the bar beside her.

"I guess he's not coming," Meggy announced around the lump in her throat. "What if he's decided I'm just too much trouble? What if he doesn't love me enough to fight for me after all?"

Cara snorted. "Trevor? The man who announced to the entire town that you were marrying him? Not a chance."

"Cara's right, Meggy." Finn pointed his beer bottle her way. "You haven't seen the last of Trevor Christos."

"If you're having second thoughts about this plan of yours, you could always tell him the truth, babe." Justin plucked a candied apple from a tray on the bar and sunk his teeth in with a crunch. "I wouldn't complain," he said around the mouthful of treat. "Even pretending I'm about to shackle myself in wedded bliss is enough to make me consider taking up a musical instrument for real and going out on an extended tour."

She smiled. "I haven't changed my mind, and you promised."

"I promised, and I'll go through with your charade." He tapped a finger to her nose. "But if he breaks my jaw, you'll owe me big time."

Cara and Finn laughed.

But she just shrugged. "I already owe you. If he breaks your jaw you can put it on my tab."

"Did you ask Elizabeth where Trevor was?" Cara asked.

She frowned and searched the room for her great-grandmother. In her Queen Elizabeth costume, she looked as if she were holding court in reality, as she conversed with three of the town's oldest and most influential residents, including Finn's great-aunt, Maive Cataldo, and Jasper and Bertie Watson.

"I asked her a few minutes ago, but she wouldn't tell me. She said she'd raised one fool and passed her blood down to another. And that if the two of us wanted to continue to play such games, she would have no part of it. Maive, Jasper, and Bertie all agreed with her."

Cara laughed, eyeing the group sitting with Elizabeth. "God. Can you imagine if the four of them teamed up together? They could terrorize entire continents."

She grinned and didn't disagree.

"You're looking a little tense there, Mother Goose." Finn winked at Shan who hurried toward the bar. "What's up?"

"Trevor just came in through the back door." She turned a worried gaze on Meggy. "He's in the kitchen, Meggy. He wants to talk to you."

"Show time!" Cara crooned.

Her heart rate took off like a race horse coming out of the gate.

Justin dropped a big hand on her shoulder. "Last chance. Are you sure you want to go through with this, babe?"

Cara scowled at Justin. "Don't try to talk her out of it." She turned back and her eyes sparkled with challenge. "He deserves to pay a price. Since he was the one who involved the whole town, he deserves to pay it in front of most of Palmerton." Her dark brows arched. "It's either this, or I go get my machete."

Justin and Finn laughed.

Meggy was too nervous to appreciate the humor. She gave Shan an apologetic smile, concerned her frantically beating heart was about to explode from her chest. "Would you mind telling Trevor I'm dancing with my fiancé, Shan?"

"Me?" Shan squeaked. "Why do I have to be the one to tell him?"

"He's not going to do anything to you. It's me he'll want to kill."

"Not to mention me." Anticipation sharpened Justin's grin.

"I'll protect you, babe." She patted his arm.

Shan threw up her hands and turned on her heel.

"Shall we?" Justin held out a hand.

She placed her damp palm in his, and he towed her onto the dance floor, sweeping her into his arms. His gaze trained toward the kitchen, he twirled her. A moment later, he dropped her into a dip and covered her mouth with his.

The crash of the kitchen door bursting open sounded above the music.

## Chapter Twenty-One

"Cooper!" Trevor barked across the distance. "Unless you want them broken, you'll take your hands off her."

A shudder went through Meggy.

Justin straightened, bringing her up with him. When she started to move away, he clamped her to his side. Arching a brow, he watched Trevor approach. "Is there a problem?"

"The only problem is yours, if you don't get your hands off my future wife," Trevor said with amazing calm, considering the murder in his eyes.

"*Your* future wife?" Justin turned a laughing gaze on Meggy. "I thought you were marrying *me*, babe."

Trevor took a threatening step forward.

She wriggled free of Justin's hold. She jammed a hand against Trevor's chest before he could reach her grinning friend. "Stop it, Trevor."

His eyes were a stormy gray as they simmered down into hers. "You wanted to have this out in public, Meggy. We'll have it out in public."

"Me? I wasn't the one who blabbed our business to the whole town." She took her own menacing step forward to poke him in the chest. "I didn't announce to the entire town that we were engaged," her voice rose with each word, "when...we...aren't!"

"What the hell was I supposed to do?" he shouted.

"You wouldn't speak to me."

Their altercation finally registered on the party guests, and the place went quiet. Over Trevor's shoulder, she caught glimpses of shocked and interested faces. She wasn't surprised to see Erin hurrying closer to the action.

"If airing your laundry for the whole town pisses you off so much, you should have come into the kitchen like I asked."

Trevor obviously didn't care who heard.

"And don't think I don't know who it was who fed the town all that bullshit about you dating this bozo?" Trevor jerked his thumb in Justin's direction.

"Bozo?" Justin coughed. "I like that!"

His sly grin gave her pause. Justin hadn't become a cop because he liked to avoid conflict, he thrived on it. And she knew from personal experience he had an uncanny knack for knowing just what buttons to push to get results. How had she forgotten that little fact?

"Can we hurry this along, babe?" He spoke in a bored voice. "We've got a plane to catch." He waggled his brows. "And a hotel suite to check into."

She grimaced. Talk about overkill.

"What's the problem here, Meggy?" Bob Calhoun came to a stop several feet away, with Carol pushing through the throng to catch him. He jerked his chin in Trevor's direction. "Is this the guy who decided you were a crook before he'd even laid eyes on you?"

"I've got this, Dad," she said on a groan.

Trevor dragged his furious gaze from Justin to give her father a belligerent stare.

"If he's harassing you," Bob continued.

"I said I've got it."

"Bob." Carol reached his side and grasped his arm. "She looks like she's got things under control. Let her handle it."

Meggy figured she must resemble a pampered poodle standing between two vicious guard dogs, when her father turned a stunned gaze on his wife and barked, "It doesn't look like she's got anything under control to me."

Carol patted his arm comfortingly. "Trust me, Bob. Your little girl knows exactly what she's doing." She sent Meggy a wink and dragged him away toward their table.

*Oh no, I don't!*

"Finn!" Finn's great-aunt, Maive, spoke in the sudden silence, "Use some muscle to clear a path in that crowd. We can't see the show from over here."

At the spatter of laughter from the crowd, she squeezed her eyes shut and decided her father was right. She had lost control of "operation payback". As if to underscore that fact, the sound of a fist striking bone had her eyes popping open to the sight of Justin sprawled on the floor at Trevor's feet. "Are you crazy?" she cried. "He's a cop. You just punched a cop!" She sank to her knees at Justin's side.

"He's an asshole," Trevor said from above them.

Horrified, she ran her fingers over the mark already appearing on Justin's handsome face. He captured her hand and held it against his bruised cheek, speaking only loud enough for her to hear. "You're on your own from here, babe." He flexed his jaw. "The bastard's got a fist like a mallet."

"I'm sorry," she whispered before rising to her feet and spinning to glare at Trevor. "You had no right to

161

hurt him!"

**** 

Trevor's temper fired on all cylinders. Brody had been amused when he'd called to report that Meggy was doing everything she could to convince the people of Palmerton she was having a hot and heavy affair with her cop ex-boyfriend. Trevor hadn't been amused. Only Elizabeth's assurances that all wasn't as it seemed with Meggy and her cop, had kept him from dropping the mess he'd found in Virginia and catching the first available flight north. Instead, he'd agreed to do nothing, giving Meggy's anger the time to run its course.

But seeing the anger in her eyes now, as she defended the man against him, had him doubting Elizabeth's assessment of the situation. The possibility Meggy really did plan to use those airline tickets Brody had mentioned made his stomach clench in panic.

*Because Meggy was only half of the equation.*

He'd been so sure she was using Justin to get a little revenge against him he hadn't stopped to consider the other man's motivations. In Trevor's experience, everyone had a price. Even an honest cop would be tempted by the kind of wealth Meggy suddenly represented. Fury exploded in his gut at the idea of the man taking advantage of Meggy's play for revenge, to make a play of his own. He glared down at Justin, who had managed to sit up on the floor.

"I don't know what kind of a scam you're running here, Cooper, but it's not going to work." Meggy's gasp registered faintly despite the angry haze gripping his mind. "Meggy may be the Ashford heir, but I can guarantee you, *you'll* never see a dime of Ashford money."

Trevor braced for a blow when Justin rose to his feet. It never came.

Meggy's cop boldly met his glare with a dismissive snort and an odd flash of sympathy in his eyes. "There's no fool like a rich fool."

"Scam?" Meggy's softly spoken word wafted to his ears.

He turned to look at her. It had been the wrong thing to say, considering their history, and he knew it the moment he saw her eyes. They'd gone flat, and her fairy face had gone still, like untouchable porcelain. But damn it, she had no idea just how completely her life had been altered. She had no idea the lengths to which people would go in their attempts to get their hands on her money. The sooner she understood that, the better.

"Why the sudden interest in marrying you, Meggy? You've known the man for years. Why is it only *now* he's discovered he's madly in love with you? The only thing that's changed is your financial status."

She stiffened and two spots of color bloomed on her white face. "And of course, you believe the only reason any man could want me would be for my bank account."

"That's not what I said." He shoved a hand through his hair

"But it's what you meant." She held up a hand to halt his denial, and her bark of laughter was harsh with derision. "God. I knew I'd been a fool. I just hadn't realized how big a fool." The smile she gave the big cop was sad, and her eyes glistened with moisture. "You're wrong about Justin. Using me to get at the Ashford money isn't his style." She turned back. "But it is *your* style, isn't it?"

His heart contracted at the bleak acceptance in her

eyes. "Meggy." He took a step toward her.

"No." She retreated from his outstretched hand. "Damn you, Trevor Christos, or whatever you're calling yourself today. Scam, you say? Of the two of us, you make the better con artist. You present yourself as a successful businessman, but you're really that pirate you dreamed of being when you were a boy. You sailed into Palmerton under false colors to protect your treasure."

She pushed by him to make her way to the bar and scrambled to reach over the top, pulling out a sheaf of papers. Spinning back, she closed the distance until they were toe to toe.

The papers hit him in the chest. He fumbled to catch them.

"Your fortune is safe from me, Trevor. That's the waiver I promised you, signed and sealed. Go pillage and plunder somewhere else."

He felt as though he'd been hit with a sledge hammer. She stood before him in her sparkling fairy costume with her jaw clenched against the quiver that threatened to break free. Her eyes, pooled with tears, broke his heart.

A fairy costume, for crying out loud. She'd worn it for him, he knew. Her choice meant something. She'd expected something of him tonight, but he'd managed to blow it without ever knowing what part he was expected to play.

His stomach clenched at the shimmer of unshed tears in her eyes. She hadn't cried before—not when she'd discovered the man she loved wasn't who she'd thought him to be, not even when she realized he'd believed her a thief. He couldn't bear it if she cried now, not when he felt the urge to weep himself.

Wearily, he dropped his head to stare at the papers in his hand. They represented the dissolution of a fortune, of *her* fortune. She thought his interest in her was about the money. She believed everything he'd said and done and felt, everything they'd shared, was just part of his plan to protect his stake in the Ashford millions.

She was wrong, of course, and staring blindly at the legal documents, his mind searched frantically for a way to prove it.

*She believes it's about the money!* His heart began to hammer in his chest, shooting a red hot stream of adrenaline through his veins. "Grandmother," he called into the silence while pinning Meggy with a steady gaze.

"Yes, darling," came Elizabeth's calm voice.

"The woman I love believes the Ashford fortune is more important to me than she is."

"So it seems."

"How long would it take your attorneys to change your will, cutting me out of it completely?" He held Meggy's gaze even as her eyes widened and she began shaking her head. "Leaving everything to your great-granddaughter?" he finished.

Elizabeth's clear voice could be heard over the sudden excited murmuring of the crowd. "They should manage it in a day or two, or I'll damned well know why."

"Will you see to it then?"

"Are you sure?"

He turned to meet his grandmother's gaze across the room. There were tears in those eyes that had watched over him as he'd grown from scared boy to grown man, eyes the same color as Meggy's, but there was pride as well. "I've never been surer of anything in my life."

Silence reigned, broken only by the ticking of the grandfather clock in the entry. Not a soul in the room dared to breathe as he turned back to Meggy.

Her eyes were closed, and she'd lost the battle with her tears. They left shiny tracks on her cheeks. She continued to shake her head.

He took the two steps needed to touch her and with a long finger curved under her chin, he lifted her face. "Look at me, fairy girl." He waited until her eyelids flickered open. "I love you. You! Do you believe it?"

She nodded.

"And *you* love me. Say it." He continued to push.

She whimpered, and her face crumbled on a fresh wave of tears, but she managed to choke out the words. "I love you, Trevor, but," she gasped on a sob, "the money, I don't want it."

"Too bad." His hand disappeared into the pocket of his slacks and reappeared with her sparkling charm bracelet shimmering in his palm. "I think you should put this back on."

She didn't argue.

As he attached the clasp at her wrist, he realized his hands were shaking. "I know it's not a ring." He spoke clearly, not caring they had an avid audience. "But it'll have to do, because you're marrying me."

She blinked at fresh tears. "I am?"

"You are. Say, 'Yes, Trevor, I'll marry you.'"

"You're very bossy," she said soberly.

He held his breath for what seemed like a lifetime as he waited for her response then had to lock his knees to keep from falling. They went weak with relief at the return of her fairy smile.

"But yes, Trevor." Her smile beamed through her tears, "I'll marry you."

Trevor stared down at her pixie face shining like the sun, and the love he saw in her crystal blue eyes took his breath away.

"Kiss the girl already," Jasper called out from the crowd, bringing a roar of laughter from friends and family alike.

With a purely male smile, Trevor kissed his fairy girl.

**A word about the author...**

Mac is a wife, mother, really young grandmother, and breast cancer survivor living her dream. Along with her husband of thirty years, a neurotic Pomeranian, and a blind cat, she lives in Phoenix because the southwest feeds her soul.

Thank you for purchasing
this publication of The Wild Rose Press, Inc.
For other wonderful stories of romance,
please visit our on-line bookstore at
www.thewildrosepress.com.

For questions or more information
contact us at
info@thewildrosepress.com.

The Wild Rose Press, Inc.
www.thewildrosepress.com

To visit with authors of
The Wild Rose Press, Inc.
join our yahoo loop at
http://groups.yahoo.com/group/thewildrosepress/